Books by *Frederick Buechner*

Novels

Non-Fiction

TREASURE HUNT

FREDERICK BUECHNER

TREASURE HUNT

Atheneum *New York* 1977

Library of Congress Cataloging in Publication Data

Buechner, Frederick, 1926–
  Treasure hunt.

  I. Title.
PZ3.B8597TT [PS3503.U257]   813'.5'4   77-4743
ISBN 0-689-10800-1

For **Bob** *and* **Betty Clayton**

TREASURE HUNT

CHAPTER ONE

GERTRUDE CONOVER turned on her cassette player, and over it came the unmistakable voice of my father-in-law Leo Bebb. It said, "The trouble with folks like Brownie is they hold their life in like a bakebean fart at a Baptist cookout and only let it slip out sideways a little at a time when they think there's nobody noticing. Now that's the last thing on earth the Almighty intended. He intended all the life a man's got inside him, he should live it out just as free and strong and natural as a bird. Now you take your—"

The speaking cut off into a noise like a vacuum cleaner, and Gertrude Conover pushed the re-wind button. Backwards at top speed, Bebb's voice became the falsetto dither of Disney mice.

Gertrude Conover said, "That was the last part, but it doesn't matter which part you start with because the thing's a regular patchwork quilt. He must have fiddled around with it off and on for weeks."

She said, "It makes you feel awfully blue to hear that voice again, doesn't it? I've been on two cruises since this was made, and I might as well have saved my money for all they helped cheer me up. I've never been one to rush from one life to the next, but there have been times I thought that without Leo Bebb to pep things up, this one couldn't end too soon to suit me."

Gertrude Conover was a Theosophist and believed in reincarnation.

I said, "He took a lot of the action with him when he checked out. There's no question about that."

Sharon said, "I've got a question. How come you never played this thing to us before? It's been a whole year."

Gertrude Conover said, "My dear, I was only told about it myself last week. I immediately asked you two down for the weekend to hear it."

It was a Saturday afternoon in June, and the three of us were out by Gertrude Conover's swimming pool in Princeton, New Jersey. Gertrude Conover was sitting in a canvas deckchair wearing one of those transparent green eyeshades that I associate with poker players in old gangster movies and holding the cassette player on her knees. Although she was in her early eighties, she looked closer to sixty-five or seventy. She had blue hair and washed-out blue eyes, and she was looking at us half over

4

her shoulder the way she tended to look at everything. Even when she walked straight toward you, she seemed to be coming on a diagonal. Sharon was lying flat on her back on the hot slates with her wet hair drying to her shoulders like seaweed, one long leg stretched out straight, and the other drawn up at the knee. I was lying on my stomach beside her. In the background you could hear the sound of the hand mower that Callaway was using to trim around under the lilacs—the hectic forward rattle and languid backward sigh that remind me always of the long summer naps of childhood.

Sharon said, "Who was the one told you about it, Gert?" and Gertrude Conover said, "I'll play it for you first and answer that afterwards."

I suppose that under different circumstances it would have made me feel blue, as Gertrude Conover predicted, to hear Bebb's voice again when I'd thought for sure that he'd stopped talking permanently. The way things were, however, it wasn't the blueness that struck me so much as the oddness of the coming together of many different things at once like the voice of Bebb and the smell of the lilacs, the sound of Callaway's mower, Sharon stretched out beside me in all her glory with the top of her bathing suit untied so her shoulders would tan properly. And there were all the different kinds of things Bebb had recorded too, a kind of oral doodling he must have killed time with at odd moments during the last weeks he had lived at Gertrude Conover's before the combined hostility of the Princeton Police, the fire insurance people and the Internal Revenue Service had forced his sensational departure.

There were a number of dead spots on the tape, passages of Bebbsian silence that buzzed like bees through the silence of our listening to him all those months later. There were noises, some that weren't identifiable and some that were—rattling papers, creaking chairs, a radio or a TV muttering away in the background. You could hear Bebb clear his throat a few times, hum, make sigh sounds. Once there were a couple of loud blasts that I took to be honking, as if he had gone out for a drive one day and taken the little machine along with him for something to talk to. Most of the time I listened to it with my eyes closed, and as each section came along I found myself picturing him as he made it.

Plump and pale he sits on the edge of his bed in his shirtsleeves with his chin in his hands not noticing that outside there is a wet spring snow falling and a cardinal on the bird feeder.

It is early morning, but he is fully dressed in his gents furnishings suit with all five points of the handkerchief showing from his breast pocket. He is staring at his Tweedledum reflection in the dresser mirror. There is no sign that his bed has been slept in.

His bald head glints in the moonlight as he stands looking out the dark window. In the rapid hush of a man at his prayers he is saying, "Robe to the cleaners. Check out the TV guarantee. Contact Fats. Read up on Battle of Princeton. See does Rexall's carry rhubarb and soda. Hemorrhoid salve. . . ."

I reach out to touch Sharon's bare foot with mine, but she does not touch me back. Through my one open eye I see that Gertrude Conover's eyeshade has turned the upper half of her face green. Some scraping sound Bebb made a year before startles a dragon fly off the diving board. It skims the turquoise water and then up across the slope of lawn toward the broad terrace of Revonoc. Revonoc is the name of Gertrude Conover's place in Princeton. It is Conover spelled backwards.

As for the tape itself, to me it was all fascinating—even the lists, the pauses, the unfinished scraps of things—because it was all Bebb, and Bebb speaking from another world, and Bebb speaking to himself, which meant that for all I knew he might at any moment lay some secret bare, some shadowy corner of those last days of his life when he recorded it. But objectively speaking, most of it was of no great significance, and I preserve here only a fraction of all there was: first, some notes he made for one of his Love Feast sermons at Alexander Hall presumably, then a couple of letters, and finally—just before the already quoted words about Brownie—a kind of testamentary passage which was to have the most far-reaching consequences for all three of us and others. I think not just of the whole crazy journey south in Gertrude Conover's Continental but all the ambiguous epiphanies, the apocalyptic confrontations, the scandalous revelations. *Had we but known*, as the old come-on goes, but of course we didn't know. We just listened to the voice of Bebb rattling on out of the past as though it was in no sense a matter of life and death at all.

The high points were as follows.

Bebb says, "The kingdom of heaven, it's like unto treasure hid in a field the which when a man hath found it, he hideth it and for joy thereof"—Bebb comes down so hard on *joy* it makes the machine rattle—"he goeth and selleth all he hath or ever hopes to hath and buyeth that field. Well, it's like you're poking around a junk shop, and inside a old humpback trunk with the lid half stove in you come across a pack of letters somebody's great grandad tied up with a string from a chum back home name of Abe Lincoln that's worth a clear five thousand bucks each if they're worth a dime. Now you tell me what a man would give to lay his hands on that trunk. Why he'd give his bottom dollar. He'd give his right arm for a treasure like that, and for the kingdom of heaven—Listen," Bebb says, "he'd give ten years, twenty years, off his life. You know why? Why because the kingdom of heaven, that's what it is. It's life. Not the kind of half-baked, moth-eaten life we most of us live most of the time but the real honest-to-God thing. Life with a capital L. It's the treasure a man spends all his born days looking for, no matter if he knows it or not. The kingdom of heaven, it's the treasure that up till a man finds it, every other treasure that comes his way doesn't amount to spit."

Bebb says, "The kingdom comes by looking for it. The kingdom comes sometimes by not looking for it too hard. There's times the kingdom comes by it looking for you."

Then one of the buzzing silences, and at the end of it, breathily, as if he's holding the microphone to his lips, "Maybe it don't come at all. Period."

8

LETTERS   The first one is to the IRS agent named Connor, who initiated proceedings against Bebb for filling out his form 1040 in the name of Jesus instead of his own name, putting down things like *the wages of sin is death* where it asked for wages and *I am the first and the last, saith the Lord,* where it asked for last name.

Bebb says, "Friend Connor, I call you friend because like the Apostle Paul said, 'Let not the sun go down upon your wrath,' Ephesians four, and the sun's going down here in Princeton, New Jersey, in more ways than one. You and that woman you got working for you have used me hard from the word go. You kept me cooling my heels in that waiting room till I missed my dinner, and when you finally let me in, you uttered all kinds of evil against me falsely. I know you can't help it hardly. You are a undersize man trying to add cubits to your stature being spiteful and mean, and that woman she is a plain woman trying to make up for it painting a pair of lips on her wouldn't fool a blind man. Connor, I'm no lily either, but I'm not a cheat. I filed like I did because every nickel of income I ever took in, I took it in for Jesus, and every nickel of out-go I ever laid out, I laid that out for Jesus too. Connor, life's too short to stay enemies. Your friend in Jesus, Leo Bebb."

The second letter is to a member of the Princeton history department who was instrumental in getting the university authorities to stop letting him stage his Love Feasts in Alexander Hall.

Bebb says, "Roebuck, that cripple boy you got you say he can't take a leak without somebody comes and pulls his pecker out for him, don't you let this spite you got

9

for the Almighty on account of that stop you asking him to make that boy whole whether you believe the Almighty's up there to hear you asking him or not. Ask him anyway. Roebuck, all the believing a man's got to do is believe it's worth the chance. Say it's only a one in a million shot there is a Almighty, what you got to lose talking to him, Roebuck? Yours truly, Leo Bebb."

I remember wondering as I lay there with the sun hot on my back if Bebb had ever gotten around to mailing the letters. I never got a letter from him myself; in fact as far as I know, I never even saw his handwriting. I never saw him asleep either, or cry. I never saw him naked. We must have shaken hands dozens of times over the years, but I have no recollection of what his handshake felt like. Once he hugged me, and I recollect that. It was when he was hiding out in the basement of a storage warehouse in lower Manhattan, and though I didn't know it then, it was the last time I was ever to see him. Bebb knew it. He had on a fancy red dressing gown he'd dug up somewhere, and throwing his arms around my shoulders, he gave me a squeeze that almost knocked my breath out.

In any case, it was at some point during the tape of the letter to Roebuck that something happened to make Gertrude Conover turn off the machine.

"Jesus," Sharon said, "what's bugging Callaway?" and I looked up to see him come running out from behind the lilacs with his head tipped back as far as it would go and a white handkerchief pressed to his black face. Sharon had sat up in such a hurry that she forgot she had undone the straps of her bathing suit top, and I remembered how startled and white her breasts looked, like another pair of eyes. Callaway was in too much of a hurry to notice them as he came tearing past, and when Sharon herself noticed, she made no big production of it, just reached up behind her neck and tied things back in place again.

"He hasn't had one of his nosebleeds for ages," Gertrude Conover said. "Sometimes all it takes is the mention of Leo Bebb's name although Callaway himself is no more aware of the connection than he is aware that in an earlier life he was the Pharaoh. Who would think to look at him now that there was a time when he had only to snap his fingers and both the Lower and Upper Kingdoms would dance attendance?"

"He's come a long way since then," Sharon said.

Gertrude Conover said, "My dear, we all of us have."

When the tape started to play again, I hoped that maybe Bebb would say something that might shed light on the climactic events of the preceding spring. The march on Nassau Hall to protest his expulsion from the Princeton Campus and the historic seizure and siege of Alexander Hall that followed it; the balloon-scattering flight in a stolen plane over the heads of the Reunion P-rade as it moved down Nassau Street; the fiery crash in the potato field—I hoped especially that Bebb might give some clue as to how much of it all he had planned out carefully in advance and how much was just happenstance. Failing that, I hoped he might reminisce about some of the other events in his life that I had always wanted to know more about. I would like to have heard him expand on how he and Lucille had come to adopt

Sharon after their own baby's death or on the five years he had spent in the pen, not to mention the event that had landed him there which I had only the most fragmentary picture of: the sunlit stucco wall out behind a Miami Beach seafood restaurant; some barefoot kids playing niggerbaby with a tennis ball; Bebb with something pale and shapeless nestled in his hand.

Bebb had never told me much about himself except a glimpse here and there, and he had never encouraged me to tell him much about myself either though God knows there were times I would have given my right arm to. The winter that Sharon and I had split up for a while, for instance; if he'd given me the faintest sign, I'd have started unloading things on him then that I'd probably be unloading on him still if he were still around to unload them on, but he never gave me the chance. Bebb was always in a hurry. You felt he couldn't let anything sidetrack him, not even the sad things that were happening that winter to his daughter Sharon, who was the apple of his eye, the one he loved more than all the rest of us put together.

It was to Sharon that the most important part of the tape was addressed and also to me, but this time it wasn't a letter. Bebb said, "Sharon, honey, this is your old Bip talking. Antonio, I'm talking to you too. I'm talking to the both of you sitting there side by side again like the Almighty intended. Little children, let us love one another because he that loveth not abideth in death. Amen. That's the whole of Scripture in a nutshell. It's the whole of everything in a nutshell. Gertrude Conover, you're welcome to listen in too. There's some ways you're the best friend I ever had, and if things had turned out different, well who knows." It was an uncanny business, and I could feel Sharon's muscles tightening where our bare arms touched.

Bebb said, "All my life I wanted to do something big for Jesus only nothing I ever did amounted to scratch. Could be the best thing I ever did for him was back when I was on the road selling Bibles where folks could read up on him for theirselves, but that wasn't big enough to suit me. I wanted to be up there in the head office—gospel-preaching, healing, revivals, the whole shebang. Talk about your missions, I set up Gospel Faith College and put in paid ads all over creation. 'Put yourself on God's payroll,' they said. 'Go to work for Jesus now.' A racket? The way they—"

Bebb broke in upon himself. He said, "Listen, was it a racket Jesus saying lay down your fishpole? Leave go your buck-saw, your manure fork, you name it, and follow me. Two-bit whores, crooks, sodomites—Jesus didn't ask for any credentials, and I didn't either. I ordained anybody answered that ad and sent in his love offering. Gospel Faith's still in business, but it's small potatoes. Everything I ever did, it was small potatoes. I'm a small potato my own self, and that's the truth of it. A man does what he can."

I could see Callaway up by the far end of the terrace. His face was tilted to the sky like a drought victim watching for rain, and he was holding his nostrils pinched tight together with one hand. Sharon was sitting with her knees clasped to her chest and staring somberly down at the ground.

Bebb said, "The grass withereth, the flower fadeth. There's no man lives forever. Whether he's done big

13

things in his life or just small, pitiful things, the time comes like a thief in the night when the show's over. A man thinks about after he's gone. He thinks about the things he never got around to doing and he wonders will there be anybody to pick up where he left off."

A tinkling sound stirred faintly in the background of the recording, and I pictured Bebb sitting there with his back to the TV which was turned on low across the room. It was playing a little song about false teeth adhesive or a gentle but effective laxative.

He said, "All the money I've got after bills and taxes if that sawed-off little penpusher in Trenton, New Jersey, leaves me with two red cents to rub together, all that, it's to come straight to you two and your kids, no strings attached, and that's that. I thought some about passing it on to Holy Love, but Herman Redpath, he pumped enough into Holy Love to keep it afloat till kingdom come, and Open Heart, well it burned down, and Love Feast, let's face it, those love feasts they're not going to last any longer than me if that long. So all the money, that's yours free and clear. But there's something else.

"There's a piece of land outside of Spartanburg, South Carolina, that belongs to me. It's down there in a place name of Poinsett that's where I was born and raised, and there's a house on it that's mine too. I don't suppose anybody's lived there going on twenty-five, thirty years, but far as I know it's still standing. It's the house I first saw the light of day in. Up till the day I got married and moved out, it was home. Now what I want to say to you is this."

As Bebb got ready to say it, something must have

gone wrong with his machine because the speed was suddenly cut way down, and his voice started coming out twice as deep and half as fast so that he sounded drugged or like a man trying to talk in the midst of a paralyzing yawn.

Dragging each word out to inordinate length, he said, "Antonio, I'm leaving that place to Sharon and you. The land and the old homestead. Both. I'm not laying anything on you what to do with it. You can sell it and use the cash. You can give it away. You can turn it into something. Any whichway. But you mind this.

"An . . . to . . . ni . . . o . . ," Bebb said, and the way my name came inching out, it was as though I was hearing the full, painful truth of it for the first time. "I want you to do something nice with that old place. And I want you to do it for Jesus."

Those fateful words.

Then the part again about Brownie's life-style being like a repressed fart. The vacuum cleaner noise cut it off in mid-sentence, and Sharon said, "Why Bopper, you're crying."

I thought she was crazy. I have never cried easily, and I wasn't crying then. I wasn't even feeling as if I might cry given half a chance. It was queer and sad in a way to hear Bebb's voice again, but it was nothing that made me feel like breaking down. I told her that.

She said, "Then what's all that running down your cheeks like rain?" and she was right. I put my hands to my face, and it was wet.

She said, "It's Leo Bebb. He has apparently affected

your eyes much the way he has affected poor Callaway's nose."

"Like an allergy," I said, and even as I said it, I could feel a new hot trickle start down. Then Gertrude Conover. It was an eery thing to see. First her eyes seemed to be swelling in size, getting goiterish and glittery in the green light of her visor, and then there we were, the two of us, looking on the outside as though our hearts were breaking whereas on the inside we were both of us going on with business as usual.

Gertrude Conover dropped the cassette player back into her knitting bag and took out a Kleenex to dab at her face. She said, "The karmic energy of that man is something to write home about. Just the sound of his voice has an effect not unlike that of peeling a Bermuda onion."

"Not on me," Sharon said, and Gertrude Conover said, "That's what you think."

Even as Sharon had spoken, it had started happening to her too; then right in the midst of it that sudden shattering, shattered smile of hers. "You've got to hand it to old Bip," she said.

That evening Gertrude Conover drove us for dinner to a place across the river in Pennsylvania not far from New Hope, and as her Continental rolled along through the green countryside, I remember thinking about the name New Hope and all the other lovely old names we have and what a pity it is we've long since stopped hearing what they meant to the people who christened their towns with them—not just hope but *new* hope.

Providence. Concord. A new *haven* safe from the high seas and punishing winds of the world. Anyway, the restaurant where she took us turned out to be in the branches of an enormous tree. There were platforms fanning out at different levels among the leaves, and tables on them with checkered tablecloths, and candles burning like fireflies. It was up there somewhere, over our *coq au vin* and beaujolais that Sharon said, "Gertrude Conover, you never did get round to telling us who it was put you on to where Bip's tape was."

Gertrude Conover looked at her in that encouraging, hopeful way she always had as though she expected you to go on and say something even better than what you'd just finished saying, but when Sharon didn't say anything more, she finally just answered the question. She said, "There's no point beating about the bush. The one who told me about Leo Bebb's tape was Leo Bebb himself."

Sharon leaned forward. She said, "You mean his ghost?"

Gertrude Conover said, "It was not a ghost."

I have never seen Sharon's face so still. It was still like a top when it's spinning so fast you can't believe it's spinning. She said, "He didn't die in the crash then?"

It was what I'd always wanted to believe, of course. That he'd baled out somehow or been thrown clear. That he'd found his way to some southsea paradise where the natives had crowned him with parrot feathers and made him their god or their king. The plane had burned up so completely that no trace of him was ever found, not so much as a gold filling or the sole of a shoe, so it was possible after all. I hung on Gertrude Conover's next words.

She said, "He never went into all that. He was obviously more interested in the future than the past, and as usual he seemed a little pressed for time."

It was a mild evening, and you could see the moon through the branches. There were several broad, shallow stairways leading down to the ground, and a waiter was sitting at the foot of one of them with his head in his hands. A bunch of eleventh grade English papers were waiting back home to be corrected—the Sutton High commencement was only a few days away—and there I was, up in a tree listening to an octagenarian theosophist with blue hair who might be telling the truth, or making it all up as she went along, or suffering from hardening of the arteries.

Gertrude Conover said, "It was after I got back from the Budapest concert at McCarter last week. They'd done the first Razoumovsky, which is my favorite. Dee dee *dum*, dee *dum*, dee *dee*. Well, it takes the wrinkles out, that's all. I was sitting out on the terrace letting the music wash back over me under the stars with a cup of hot ovaltine and some graham crackers when suddenly I heard this voice beside me saying, 'Long time no see, Gertrude Conover,' and of course I knew in a second who it was. I would recognize that voice anywhere. I said, 'Leo, you're a sight for sore eyes,' and he said, 'I could use one of those graham crackers, Gertrude Conover, if you've got one to spare.' "

I said, "Do you mean he was alive like you and Sharon and me, the way the three of us in this tree are alive right this minute?"

She said, "Oh I would say a good deal more alive than that. Under certain circumstances, the cosmic batteries can recharge very rapidly."

I said, "How did he look?" and she said, "Not a bit fuzzy around the edges, if that's what you mean. Round. Clean. Much the way he's always looked. I had several grahams left, and he ate them all."

"What did you talk about?" Sharon said, and she looked at me as she said it and narrowed her eyes at me, just the merest flicker with nothing else in her face moving.

Gertrude Conover said, "He did most of the talking, and it didn't last long. He told me the tape was under the Hudson Bays in his old closet, and it was. He said he knew you didn't even know the South Carolina place existed because he never got around to listing it separately in his will, and he's got his heart set on your doing something about it, you especially, Antonio. He said he should have gone down there himself years ago, but he never got around to it. If you ask me, the trip would have stirred up a lot of old memories he'd as soon have let be. The childhoods of Leo Bebb have almost never been happy ones, and I could tell he was relieved as soon as the subject changed. We parted soon afterwards."

I said, "I'm trying to picture it, Gertrude. I'm trying to see him walk away across the lawn or get into a car and drive off."

She said, "Well I'm afraid I can't help you with that because I was the one who left first. What with the Razoumovsky and the ovaltine and the surprise of seeing him, I suddenly felt so exhausted I said good night and went straight up to bed. He understood perfectly. Besides, he'd done what he came for."

"Did you shake hands goodbye?" Sharon said. "Did

you ever the whole time he was there touch him with your own two hands, Gertrude Conover?"

A little gust of air rustled the leaves and bent the flame of our candle sideways. Gertrude Conover took a sip of her beaujolais and then said, "My dear, a great many lives have come and gone since the last time I touched Leo Bebb with my own two hands."

I said, "What was the last thing he said before you left?"

She said, "The last thing he said before I left was 'See you in the funny papers.' Within ten minutes of that I was in dreamland."

CHAPTER TWO

BEBB HAD SAID, "Antonio, I want you to do something nice with that old place. And I want you to do it for Jesus." The question was what was I supposed to do with it? When was I supposed to start? How could I be sure Jesus would approve?

Beyond that, there were cloudier questions. Was Gertrude Conover reporting an actual encounter with Bebb in the flesh? There were the graham crackers after all. Or was it Bebb's ghost unable to rest in peace until the Poinsett matter was settled to his satisfaction? She never saw him arrive or depart; as nearly as I could tell, she hadn't actually *seen* him very well at all. Or was she just wandering in her mind? Sharon said, "Antonio, she can't hardly even get the seams of her hose straight any more. Sometimes when you try and talk with her, it's like she's a million miles away."

Yet the last time we saw her before setting off for Sutton, she gave no such impression. She spread a road atlas out on the library table and showed us the route she had marked in with a red crayon. She said, "We could take the Chesapeake Bay Bridge and go by way of Washington. We could spend the night there and see the sights. Then we could proceed at a leisurely pace through the Virginia countryside. The horses. The old houses. Have you ever visited Monticello? Well, we could take our time and see anything we felt like. Callaway would enjoy driving us. He is a southerner born and bred." Gertrude Conover was a world traveler as well as a theosophist. Together she and Bebb had climbed the Acropolis by moonlight, had dangled head down like bats to kiss the Blarney Stone.

She said, "As for the Jesus part, why couldn't you get Brownie to join forces with us? He might have some good ideas about the sort of thing Jesus would go for." Brownie, otherwise Laverne Brown, was Bebb's sometime assistant, factotum, stooge, who was now in charge of the Church of Holy Love outside Houston.

Later that day on the way back to Connecticut, Sharon said, "I don't know, Bopper. The whole thing seems like a wild goose chase to me. Bip said himself nobody's lived there going on twenty-five years. You ask me, all that's left is just a hole full of old corncobs where the outhouse was. I vote we sell out like he said and give the money to UNICEF. Why wouldn't that suit Jesus just fine?"

I got my papers corrected finally. I sat through Commencement watching the girls in their long dresses and high heels teeter up for their diplomas, the boys in their bellbottoms and Elizabethan tresses. Our six year old son Bill gave a terrible cold to his baby sister Lucy, who treated us all to a week of sleepless nights during which I spent so much time helping walk her back to sleep that all day long for a while I tended to break into the same bouncing stride. I spent the first day of vacation working on a six foot mobile I'd put up in the back yard a few years earlier. One of the legs of the tripod it hung from had split, and I had to replace some strips of lathing. I'd made the thing myself, an A-shaped enigma of wooden cubes, tongues, dowels, and I hated to see it drop slowly to pieces before my eyes.

Life went on much as usual, in other words, but off and on I kept thinking about Bebb and the mission he'd charged me with. I dreamed about him once, or at least he made a brief appearance at the end of a dream about something else. It was raining, and I was standing out in some kind of roughly circular field trying to dig a hole, but every time I took another shovelful, the rain and mud started filling it back up again until my arms got so tired I could hardly make them move. Then suddenly, way off in the distance, I saw Bebb. He was strolling along in his tight black raincoat and Happy Hooligan hat. I called out to him, and I could tell he'd heard me because he stopped and looked in my direction, but when I called out to him again to come give me a hand with the digging, he started walking away. I tried to follow him, but by that time I was up to my knees in the hole I'd been working at. Then I noticed that Sharon was there beside me in her yellow plastic rainhat. She said, "It's just like I told you, Antonio. You're just digging your own grave." It came out like the punch-line of an old family joke. Every word of it was rich with comic associations, including the two occurrences of the word 'just,' and I laughed so hard that laughter became the bridge I got out of the dream on. When I woke up there were tears of it in my eyes.

That same week I also saw a home movie that had Bebb in it. It was a reel I'd taken with the Bell and Howell he'd given me the summer he took Sharon and me to Europe with him, and I ran it off one of the nights when I was taking my turn with the baby. The projector was still set up from the last time I'd used it, and sitting with the baby over my shoulder like a hot water bottle, I started the past flickering away through the 3AM dark.

There was my nephew Tony in chewed-off blue jean shorts and no shirt working out with his weights in the back yard. There was my son Bill strapped onto a merry-go-round horse at Playland, that small, bewildered face spinning around and around through the gilded shadows. Sharon was sitting on the green grass in her black leotards. With both her arms stretched out sideways like wings, she leaned forward farther and farther until finally her forehead touched one knee.

Then Bebb.

He is standing at the door of Open Heart. Above his

head the life-size glass cross is lit up inside with OPEN on the horizontal part and HEART coming down through it where the E is. There is a red heart after the N in OPEN to make it symmetrical. He is wearing his maroon preaching robe and shaking hands with the congregation as they come filing out. I recognize the man with the white cane who said he was a cousin of Harry Truman's and the woman with red hair who sometimes brought a pet gerbil in a cage to the services. There are also some black women in white gloves and Sunday hats. Bebb suddenly notices me taking his picture and starts to wave. As he does so, he unknowingly knocks one of the black ladies' hats crooked. I zoom in on him at this point, and the nearer he comes, the wider my Optronic Eye opens until his face on the screen becomes not only much bigger than life but about ten times brighter. At the farthest reach of the zoom, the features slip out of focus and the face turns into an incandescent blur that nearly fills the screen. It is so bright that the baby stirs on my shoulder. Then a grid-shape snaps across it, branding it like a waffle iron. The reel ends.

Sharon is behind me in a pair of my pajamas and reaches down to lift the warm baby away. She says, "You're fretting yourself sick over this, Bopper. Do like Gertrude Conover says and go see Brownie, hear. That way you can settle what to do once and for all."

A dark snake-like thing starts uncoiling down in one corner of the screen as the projector bulb scorches a hole in the film, and I switch it off just in time to keep Bebb's face from going up in flames.

*   *   *

I couldn't have picked a worse time for my visit to Brownie although when I suggested it over the phone, he said I couldn't have picked a better. It was to be the weekend of Rose Trionka's wedding to Johnson Badger's problem nephew Buck, and all the way from Texas I could hear the emotion in Brownie's voice as he told me that it promised a new era of peace and harmony for the Indians of the Redpath Ranch. These Indians were the relatives, friends, girl friends, and miscellaneous hangers-on of the late Herman Redpath, who had built the Church of Holy Love for Bebb back in the days when Bebb had maintained the oil-rich old sachem's potency by a daily laying on of hands. Brownie told me that for years there had been bad blood between the Trionkas and the Badgers and that was what made the union of Rose and Buck so providential. He said, "It is providential that you will be there to give them your blessing too. It is the Montagues and the Capulets all over again, dear." As water to a fish, so sweetness and light were to Brownie—sweetness like his after-shave, light like the light that flashed from his glasses with their tortoise shell brows which in conjunction with his Sears Roebuck choppers gave him the smile of a man finding agonized relief from a severe case of constipation.

He met me at the Houston airport in a Hawaiian sport shirt, sandals and bobby socks, and on the drive back to the ranch I told him about how we had discovered the existence of Bebb's property in South Carolina and how I hoped maybe he could give us some tips on the kind of thing Jesus might enjoy having us do with it. I told him how Gertrude Conover had suggested maybe some of us could drive down and look the place

26

over. I was on the point of telling him also about Gertrude Conover's report that she had actually *seen* Bebb the night she had come back from hearing the first Razoumovsky with her wrinkles taken out, but I thought better of it. Brownie listened sympathetically enough, taking his hand off the wheel from time to time and pressing my arm to show me that he was with me all the way, but I had the feeling not only that his mind was on Rose Trionka's wedding the whole time but that he was making some sort of effort to keep it there. I had the feeling that the things I was telling him were somehow a threat to his peace, so I stopped short of telling him that maybe Bebb was still alive and let him turn the conversation back to the wedding instead. I remember the royal blue sport shirt he was wearing with a tangerine sunset printed on it and dark sweat stains spreading out from under his arms like the approach of night.

We entered the Redpath Ranch through the two totem poles on either side of the main gate and stopped first at the greenhouse to pick up a basket of white gladiolas because Brownie was afraid there mightn't be enough at Holy Love. Then on past the concrete service buildings, past John Turtle's Tom Thumb golf course, and on to the sauna bath where there were two or three naked Indians asleep on deck chairs out front. Brownie said, "They're like children, dear. They don't mean any harm by it." We drove straight on through the stucco and tiled-roof residential section without stopping, but I recognized the house where Bebb had lived with the porch on which Lucille had rocked herself to death one night while Brownie, oblivious to what was going on, read her Scripture. I recognized the house that had once been Herman Redpath's with its two-story living room to give height for the organ pipes. A skinny boy with a flower between his teeth was driving an electric golf cart toward Herman Redpath's swimming pool and waved at Brownie as we drove by. Brownie said, "That's Noah Seahorn's boy, Elk. He's a rainmaker."

I said, "Have you ever seen him make rain?"

Brownie pulled slowly into the circular drive that led to Holy Love and said, "There's lots of things down here I've learned to close my eyes to."

Herman Redpath had built Holy Love to look like the Alamo. Four or five Cadillacs were pulled up out front and a red carpet had been rolled down as far as the bottom of the stone steps where a couple of Indians in shorts and T shirts were sweeping the walk before rolling it the rest of the way. There were men on ladders stringing crepe paper streamers over the entrance and down from the tops of the taller cedars like maypoles. In one of the Cadillacs some hard rock was turned up high, and by his pussycat moustache I recognized Harry Hocktaw as the one who was stretched out on the hood with his bare feet flat against the windshield, keeping time with a gourd full of dried seeds. Chock chuck chuck chickchick, chock chuck, chock.

Brownie had barely gotten out of the car when Rose Trionka's mother Bea swept down on him with her hair up in rollers and a yellow Mother Hubbard that fell from her fat shoulders like sunshine down the Capitol dome. She said, "Violet's puked on the altar. Lily says she stuck her finger down her throat for spite. Put it down, you dumb fart!" Her great breasts tossing like shipwrecks, she elbowed her way to a tub of azaleas that was moving along on brown legs.

Brownie said, "Violet's the oldest Trionka sister and the only one not yet married, but she would never have done a thing like that for spite." His smile hung at half mast as he paused to let two men carrying a harp pass between us. He said, "Sometimes just heartbreak is enough to make us puke, dear. I better go see."

I followed him into the church but hung around under the balcony while he squeezed down the center aisle past the men vacuum cleaning. The chancel was crowded with flowers—drifts of them bordering the shallow steps and ropes of them twined around the columns of the pulpit. With a wreath of white chrysanthemums around its neck, the big altar cross looked as if it had just come in first at Hialeah. The fragrance was overpowering, but it did not quite drown out Violet.

As I stood there waiting for Brownie, someone came up behind me and with a surgeon's deftness grabbed the top of my underpants and gave them a sharp, upward tug. It was John Turtle, his black hair plastered down flat, his teeth framed in gold like cufflinks. I said, "You haven't lost your touch, Joking Cousin."

"Hey there, cousin," he said. "How the hell you been anyhow?"

"Win a few, lose a few," I said. I was still trying to dislodge my underpants. "What you been doing with yourself?"

"Same old thing," John Turtle said. He gestured vigorously with his right hand.

I said, "Big wedding today."

"Big Rose," he said. "Big tits." He reached out and put both his hands on my shoulders. He cocked his head

29

to one side and gave me a glassy, clinical stare. "Nice seeing you, man," he said. "Last time was old Leo's funeral."

"You danced," I said. Crouching and barefoot on the potato field, he'd padded around and around like a dog circling in for a crap, then suddenly grabbed Gertrude Conover around the waist and held her up at arms' length like a child at a hanging. At Herman Redpath's funeral he hadn't danced but he had taken a leak into the open coffin where the old chief was lying with a Navajo blanket tucked around him and salt stuffed up his nostrils and his rear end and butter on his legs. I had never seen John Turtle perform at a wedding before.

I said, "I hope you're going to behave yourself today, Joking Cousin." With his hands on my shoulders, his face was so close that it was hard to see it whole, just separate parts of it—a bony, indented cheek, a narrowed eye.

He said in falsetto, "I hope you're going to behave yourself today, Joking Cousin." He drew me a little closer to him, and even in competition with the flowers and poor Violet's puke, his smell was something to be conjured with. Hair oil, sweat, horse were only the outer edges of it. Then he changed the position of his hands on my shoulders.

He switched the hand that had been on my right shoulder to my left and the hand that had been on my left shoulder to my right so that his bare arms made an X of flesh between us. He didn't say anything. He just let the smell sink in and the X of his crossed arms and the feeling of my underpants, which were not yet entirely unwedged. One of his gold-framed teeth glistened.

Whatever the Joking Cousin's joke was, I got the idea that it was very old and famous and deadly serious. Over his shoulder I could see Brownie beckoning me to join him down front.

Everybody came to the wedding, of course. Badgers and Trionkas, Hocktaws and Seahorns, Shoptalls, Redpaths, Turtles and Poles—there wasn't a pew with as much as two inches to spare. Undertaker chairs were set up in the side aisles, and even the balcony was overflowing. While people were getting seated, music was produced by Lizard Shoptall at the organ and Lou Emma Pole riding the harp sidesaddle—*Indian Love Call, Rose Marie, The Anniversary Waltz*. The stained glass windows blazed in the afternoon sun. Old friends hailed each other. Escaped from their families, small children toddled up and down the aisle. Babies drowsed or wailed at their mothers' breasts. Maudie Redpath, going on one hundred and twelve, was wheeled to her place in a chair with red, white and blue streamers laced through the spokes. Bea Trionka in tangerine satin was led down the aisle by John Turtle and sank into the front pew on the Trionka side like the setting sun.

The bridal procession entered to *Lohengrin*. The bride's two sisters came first, Lily about eight months gone and Violet still pale and unsteady with her circlet of gardenias slightly askew on her slippery black curls. They carried dozens of long-stemmed roses the color of frozen custard, with English ivy trailing as far as their knees, and the aisle was just wide enough to accommodate the two of them abreast. Rose herself followed on the arm of an elderly man who at first glance could have been Herman Redpath risen from the dead but was identified for me as his cousin Seahorn Redpath from Laguna Beach. He didn't stand much taller than Rose's armpit and like his late cousin had skin drawn so tight that he couldn't get his lips to close properly over his teeth. As he hesitation-stepped forward, the overhead lights swam across his shiny brown scalp like goldfish. And beside him Rose, but Rose so heavily veiled in virginal white on the arm of her tiny escort that it wasn't until later that I saw her plain. Surrounded by braves at the altar steps, Buck Badger awaited her up to his crotch in flowers.

Brownie prefaced the ceremony with a short homily based on the text "It is better to marry than to burn." Robed in white with a robin's egg blue stole around his neck that had Holy embroidered in silver down one side of it and Love embroidered in gold down the other, he explained that the text was almost universally misunderstood as a slur on matrimony. On the contrary, he said, diligent study revealed that *burning* did not refer to unsatisfied lust as commonly supposed but had to do with the practice of making burnt offerings. According to Brownie, what the Apostle Paul was saying was that although to make burnt offerings got you high marks in heaven, for a young couple like Rose and Buck to offer themselves to each other in holy matrimony got higher marks still. Brownie said, "Taking it back to the original tongue, what this scripture really means is not just it is better to marry than to burn but it is *even* better."

Brownie gazed down at the wedding party as he finished, but his glasses were so steamed up that it is doubtful he could see them.

He then proceeded to conduct things in the regulation manner. Lily took Rose's bouquet for her and placed it beside her own on the great protrusion of her lavender chiffon belly. John Turtle gave the bride away with a face so straight it was crooked. Bea Trionka muffled her emotion in a corsage the size of a cabbage, and as she thrashed around I could see where in her distraction she had forgotten to take out one of the rollers. Buck Badger got the ring on his bride's finger without fumbling it, and then, as flash bulbs went off all through the congregation, he raised her veil like the flap of a tepee and kissed her.

What happened next happened so quickly that I could not see how it was done, but all of a sudden the Joking Cousin scrambled up the steps from one side and Buck Badger closed in from the other side, and the next moment there she was, all three hundred pounds of her, floating in the air above us. I can still see her enthroned there, piled high in the air like whipped cream, like pastry. I see still that round, flat face with the black hair looped down over one eye, that dim, crazy little smile. The whole front of the church was ablaze with her. Ushers and bridesmaids staggered backwards shielding their eyes. Stained glass windows shook in their frames. It was the sheer featherbed whiteness of her that was so dazzling, all those tumbled flounces and petals of bosomy white that were Rose.

For a moment the whole church held its breath. Then Lizard Shoptall at the organ and Lou Emma Pole at the harp struck up *Que Sera, Sera,* and waving and smiling and squealing Rose Trionka Badger came down out of the chancel adorned for her husband like the heavenly city itself and went floating up the aisle a good six feet off the ground. I suppose there must have been people carrying her, but I swear I can't remember any. As far as I could tell she floated up through that canyon of Indians as much under her own power as white clouds on a summer sky.

That evening Brownie said, "I wish I could believe that somehow Mr. Bebb was looking down from the hereafter and saw it all," and I said, "I thought you could believe two or three things like that before you even had breakfast, Brownie." As soon as I said it, I wished I hadn't.

I remember a Halloween pumpkin we kept on the mantle too long one year, and how after a while the face started to go lopsided and the lid caved in and pumpkin juice started rolling down the cheeks. And so with Brownie. The smile stayed relentlessly in place, but all around it everything else started falling to pieces. He said, "I wouldn't want it to get around, dear, but the truth of it is I'm afraid I've lost my faith."

We were sitting out on his porch in our shirtsleeves. It was a breathless, heavy dusk, and the ice in our iced tea had all melted so that it was tepid and watery and tasted like snuff. From off in the distance the electric carillon of Holy Love sent *Now the Day Is Over* drifting toward us.

Brownie said, "I never had a child of my own, but it

always seemed as though maybe having faith wasn't all that different a thing. It seemed as though faith was like somebody to take care of you when you got old. A shoulder to lean on when the shadows lengthened and your work was done. A hand to hold. Now it's like I had a child once but it's died. There are times I don't know as how I can keep on going."

I said, "How did it happen, Brownie?"

He mopped around under his chin and back of his neck with his paper napkin, then leaned back in his rocker and I wondered if it was the same rocker Lucille had died in. He said, "It came on gradual, like cancer. First a little pain here, a little dark spot there. I made out like it wasn't happening. Maybe if it had been caught in time, something could have been done about it. I don't know."

"Maybe something can still be done about it," I said, but Brownie wasn't listening.

He said, "Of course when Mr. Bebb passed on, that was part of it. He raised me from the dead in Knoxville, Tennessee, dear. That was many years ago and you know the story. He was forever telling me he should have saved himself the trouble. He said I never really lived the life he'd gotten back for me, just shoved . . . just shoved it up my you-know-what and sat on it. He said hurtful things like that for my own good. He was my Rock of Gibraltar, and when he went, it seemed like he took my faith with him."

It was like driving past an accident. I tried not to look at Brownie as he spoke, but most of the time I couldn't help myself.

He said, "Another thing. I have carnal desires like

everybody else, dear. Maybe you wouldn't believe it to look at me, but I've had many opportunities for backsliding in that direction here on the ranch. These Indians, they don't mean any harm by it, but lots of times they don't care a fig what they do or who they do it with just so long as they get a chance to do it. It's like when you've got a healthy young appetite, you'll take anything that's put before you. I've always resisted these temptations because of my faith. I've passed up things that . . . joys. . . ." He took off his glasses and rubbed his eyes with his thumb and forefinger. He said, "Now I ask myself this question. All these precious things I've given up for Jesus, what have I got to show for it?"

I said, "Brownie, your interpretations of Scripture bring lots of people comfort and hope."

He said, "Scripture says, 'Cast thy bread upon the waters for thou shalt find it after many days.' I have cast my whole life upon the waters, and it's sunk out of sight like a stone."

"Nobody knows you've lost your faith, Brownie," I said. "You can keep on helping people anyway. That way you might get it back again."

He said, "You don't know how it feels to say things you don't believe any more. It's like a woman with a dead baby inside her."

It was *Abide with Me* that came fluttering dimly toward us through the deepening twilight now. By this time Brownie's face was little more than a pale blur.

He said, "Scripture says where your treasure is, there shall your heart be also. The trouble is my treasure's turned out to be a bad check. Spiritually speaking, I don't have a nickel left to my name."

36

I said, "You've still got your warm and generous heart, Brownie."

Brownie reached out and softly squeezed my arm. "I shouldn't burden you with my problems, dear," he said. "You've got problems of your own."

We sat in silence for a while, just the creaking of Brownie's rocker and the distant bells. I thought of Gertrude Conover out on the dark terrace of Revonoc and how suddenly Bebb had appeared. I thought of the way Bebb would have worked Brownie over if he'd appeared there to us—*Brownie, the most faith you ever had was just one part faith to nine parts Aqua Velva. No use to cry over a pitiful thing like that.* It would have given Brownie another pain to take his mind off the pain he was rocking away with in Lucille's chair. But Bebb's way wasn't my way, and I couldn't think of any approach of my own to use on him instead until it occurred to me that I still hadn't told him how Gertrude Conover thought she had seen Bebb, so I told him. I tried to tell him in a way that would leave it up to him, as Gertrude Conover's account had left it up to me, to decide for himself whether it was Bebb or Bebb's ghost she had seen, and when he questioned me on the point, I said, "Brownie, I asked her the same question. I said did she mean he was alive the way she and I were alive, and all she said was she hoped he was more alive than that. You take it from there."

It stopped Brownie's rocking anyway, and I pressed my advantage.

I said, "Brownie, you need a change. You need to see new places and new people, and you need to stop taking your spiritual temperature all the time." I thought of echoing Bebb's image and talking about shoving a spiritual thermometer up but decided against it.

I said, "The trouble with your faith is you've tired it half to death just worrying about it. Come on down to Poinsett with me. We'll go for Bebb and Jesus both. We'll make a vacation of it."

I was so carried away by my own persuasive powers that for the first time I felt something almost like enthusiasm for the venture myself. Sharon could come too. We could park the children somewhere. It would beat just hanging around Sutton all summer putting my six-foot mobile in shape and keeping the grass mowed. If Brownie's problem was that he'd lost his faith, mine was more or less that I'd never had one to lose that amounted to much, so like the man who hit pay dirt plowing his field, maybe we'd both stumble on something down there. But I could tell my words hadn't grabbed Brownie. He still wasn't rocking, but that was about it. Then I was inspired.

I said, "Who knows if she really saw Bebb or not. Chances are she's not all that sure herself. But just suppose she did. Stranger things have happened. And if so, it could be what we'll find in Poinsett if we go is Bebb. Maybe that's why he wants us down there."

Bebb holing up in the cellar of his mouldering homestead, broke and friendless. Bebb in disguise, the Man with a Thousand Faces. For all I knew, Bebb as the Phantom of the Opera, disfigured, crippled even, by his narrow escape from the burning plane. No such fantasy had crossed my mind before—I was summoning it up purely for Brownie's sake—but once summoned, it came to life for me.

I said, "Jesus, Brownie. Suppose he's in bad trouble and needs our help?"

Brownie's face kept changing shape like ectoplasm as I tried to read it through the darkness. When he spoke, he fitted his words to the sound of the old hymn. "When other helpers fail and comforts flee," he said, "Help of the helpless, oh abide with me."

I said, "How about it, Brownie?"

I could hear the sound he made taking a swallow of his watery, tasteless tea. He said, "Let me put it this way, dear. I don't suppose I've got anything to lose I haven't lost already."

CHAPTER THREE

I DON'T SUPPOSE that my life before I got married was ever as simple as it came to seem afterwards, but the way I remember it anyway, if I felt like doing something in those days, I just got up and did it. I had no job to tie me down—my various stabs at novel-writing, journalism, the construction of take-apart scrap-iron sculpture, gave me if nothing else the advantage of being able to drop them at a moment's notice. With both my parents dead since my childhood and my twin sister Miriam well able to take care of herself—she handled her marriage, her divorce and her death all with a minimum amount of help from me, I'm afraid—I had nobody dependent on me except for a cat named Tom, who, though he smolderingly resented every hour he had to spend caged up at the vet's whenever I took off for somewhere, knew which side his bread was buttered on and held his tongue. It's true that for six or seven years I had an *understanding* with a stately girl named Ellie Pierce, who promoted noble causes and played the piano beautifully for me alone, but even if she secretly felt I should have tailored my life more to her liking, she would never have dreamed of saying so. So if it had been back in my bachelor days that I decided to take off for Poinsett, South Carolina, I would have just packed my bag and taken off. But those days were long since gone and maybe never existed in the first place.

"This is the dog / That worried the cat / That killed the rat / That ate the malt / That lay in the house that Jack built," the old rhyme goes, and in much the same way one complication led to another as I tried to organize my departure. There was the question first as to whether or not Sharon would come along, and just in itself, let alone in what it gave rise to, that was complicated enough. There was a time when she would have leapt at any excuse for dropping like hot potatoes such few motherly chores as she actually attended to—Miriam's older boy, Chris, who lived with us for a while, took such marvelous care of Bill as a baby that Sharon was free to devote herself almost entirely to her yoga lessons, speed-reading lessons, guitar lessons and so on—but after the rapid sequence of our six month separation, the death of Bebb, and the birth of Lucy, all of this changed. She gave up her lessons, gave up her share of the health food shop that she'd started with that grizzled little well of loneliness, Anita Steen, and grabbed on to motherhood like a raft in a storm. So for her own sake as well as for the children's she hung back for a while from letting go, and at the same time I hung back from urging her to. More complications. I wanted her with me, that sleepy-limbed, somber-eyed girl with the caught-red-handed smile, wanted her to battle with, bed down with, keep my bearings by, but at the same time I didn't for one minute want her to think I was setting too much store by it. When a marriage cracks like a plate and is glued together again, of all the things you've got to be careful about, the first is to look as if you aren't being careful about any of them. So she held back from saying she'd come and I held back from persuading her until it was finally Bebb in his way who brought us together just as he'd brought us together the first time in Armadillo, Florida, by leaning on his horn to hustle her out of his Charles Addams manse in a pair of tight white slacks and a shirt the color of raspberry ice. The second time was when she'd gone back to Florida with our son Bill and I was living on tap-water instant at Mrs. Gunther's boarding house in Sutton, Connecticut. That time he did the trick simply by getting himself into such a mess that we had to pool our resources, such as they were, to try to get him out of it. This third time it was not something he did but something he'd never gotten around to doing. She said, "You know something, Bip never told me an awful lot about who his kin were or where he came from any more than he ever told me about me and where I came from if he even knew. So to hell with it, I'm going to go down with you and have a look for myself. There's got to be somebody who'll mind the kids while we're

42

gone." The question was who. Another complication.

The ones we finally hit on were my nephew Tony Blaine and his wife Laura, who lived in Manhattan. We asked them if they'd come stay while we were gone, and when they said they'd love to, it sounded as if they really meant it. What could have been less complicated than that? Except that it was complicated. To start with, Laura had a good job as hygienist in the office of a Park Avenue dentist and would have to commute back and forth from Sutton, but that raised no problems because she'd be there to get breakfast and back in time to get supper and in the meanwhile Tony would be able to keep an eye on the kids since it so happened that he was between jobs. That was what raised the problems. Poor Tony, my namesake and nemesis, that handsome, feckless, star-crossed boy who had risen to dizzy heights as track star, bon vivant, and man about town his senior year at Sutton High only to drift more or less earthwards ever since. In the year since he'd moved to New York and married Laura, he'd worked as a supermarket stock boy, a clerk in the necktie department at Brooks Brothers, an orderly in a Presbyterian old peoples' home, and on the side had gotten an occasional job modeling things like terrycloth jump suits, Irish gillies' hats and sunglasses for good measure. At twenty-four he could still think of himself as looking the field over till he turned something up that really suited him, and with Laura's salary together with what I always suspected must be an occasional handout from his older brother Chris, who worked in a Wall Street brokerage firm and could touch nothing without turning at least its edges to gilt, he could tell himself that he could afford to keep on looking things

43

over indefinitely. But I had a feeling these illusions would be harder to sustain in the workaday reality of Sutton than in the dream-spawning city. Laura would leave for work, and Tony would not leave. She would go off to earn money cleaning people's teeth, and he would stay home to deal not only with the children but with the hard fact that if he and Laura were ever to have children of their own, he would have to settle down to something permanent so they could afford it. "Christ, Tono," he said to me once, "what's an ex-jock like me good for? The best offers I've had are from some of the queers you run into in the modeling scene. One of them offered me a hundred bucks an hour just to pose for him bareass and don't think there haven't been times I've considered it."

So he was the man all tattered and torn, I suppose, with Laura the maiden all forlorn, and so on back to the rat, the cat, and finally the house that Jack built which was our house, Sharon's and mine, the place where the final complication lay buried. This was that during the bleak period when Tony and I were sharing a can at Mrs. Gunther's—this was before his marriage and during the hiatus in mine—Tony went to a flop of a New Year's Eve party that Sharon gave and when it was over, stayed on to spend the night with her accidentally, apologetically almost, as her lover. He told me about it himself in time, as eventually Sharon did too, and somehow we not only all survived it, the three of us, but even managed to come out of it with the wiring between us more or less intact. Sharon and I got back together again, Tony eventually got Laura, and after a while it came to seem as if no such thing had ever happened. Except that, with the plodding literalness of things, it had happened, and to remind us that it had there was the possibility that the true father of our daughter Lucy was not me but Tony.

I don't know how much this was something Tony brooded about as a possibility, but when he and Laura arrived with their bags the evening before Sharon and I were to set out for the south, I can't believe that it didn't at least cross his mind. We led the two of them upstairs to show them where they would be staying, where the dirty diapers went, and so on, and we had just started trooping downstairs again—I see us suspended there between floors as between incarnations with Sharon leading the way and Tony bringing up the rear—when all of a sudden our son Bill came staggering down the hall with his baby sister cradled precariously in his arms. Tony leaped to the rescue. He ran back upstairs, snatched the baby up, and stood there looking down at her with his face gone all haywire and x's where his eyes should have been like Krazy Kat hit with a brick. "Well, I'll be goddammed," he said, "I'll be goddammed" and it was only after he'd said it two or three times more that I realized it was probably the first time he had ever actually held her and that though he had seen her before, he was in a way seeing her for the first time and seeing God knows what all else besides. Then Sharon said, "Hand her on down to her mama, hear," and I remember the awkward way I had to lean sideways as he conveyed her down over the bannister to her mother. I remember how Laura and I were compressed together there for a moment or two beneath the London Bridge of their reaching arms.

It was an awkward evening generally, as I look back

on it, and partly at least because before it was over, our roles got turned around somehow. Sharon and I with our bags all packed to make our early start the next morning became the guests, and I had the sense of Tony and Laura marking time like restless hosts until we were gone. There was an awkwardness too in Laura's having known me for so long as Mr. Parr—she had been in Tony's class at Sutton High and had me for English her senior year—that she had a hard time calling me either Tono the way Tony did, or Antonio or Bopper like Sharon, so that most of the time she called me nothing at all, which made me feel all the more ghostly and guest-like. Bill was the only one of us who seemed to have his feet on the ground, and even as he tottered around sleepily among us in a space helmet after supper, his presence was so stabilizing that I found myself dreading the moment Sharon would take him up to bed. When the moment finally came, she was already half way up the stairs with him when he called down that he wanted Tony to carry him the rest of the way and Tony was off like a shot, the whole house rattling as he pounded up after them. This left Laura and me alone together in the living room with poor Laura having no name to call me by when she finally said, "Maybe it's time we let you and Sharon go to bed now too. You've got a long drive ahead of you tomorrow," and I said, "I hope you'll like it here while we're gone. It will be a change anyway," and she said, "A change is always nice, and then it's nice when you get back home again too." It was like trying to play tennis without a ball.

I said, "Bill shouldn't give you any trouble. He's also pretty helpful if you have any trouble with the baby," and she said, "Oh I don't think it's any of it going to be like any trouble."

She was sitting across the room by a bridge lamp with the light of it in her hair, and she was looking down at her hands as she talked, frowning at them with her eyebrows raised as though there were several things about her hands that puzzled her. I thought of all the months she had sat at the back of my classroom looking much the same way with her lashes dark against her cheeks, not wanting to catch my eye for fear I'd ask her some question she didn't know the answer to.

Upstairs there was the sound of Sharon's voice followed by Tony's locker-room laugh snapping through it like a damp towel, the patter of Bill's bare feet across the ceiling and a thump in the pipes as a faucet was turned on.

"It makes me think of *Dear Brutus*," I said. "Remember that one?"

She said, "I remember the title. It was Sir Peter Barrie, I remember."

"Sir Peter Pan," I said. "Sir James Barrie. It was the one where everybody got a chance to—"

"Now I remember," she said and, knowing an answer finally, raised her eyes. "It was this enchanted forest and they all had a chance to see how things might have turned out if they'd done something different in their lives."

"Like those two upstairs a couple, and you and me down here a couple. It was just something that crossed my mind," I said, but as soon as I'd tossed it across the empty place between us, it became more than I'd ever bargained for. For a moment or two then there was no empty place between us with her looking across at me out of her life and me looking across at her out of my life, the separate lives we had each of us lived touching awkwardly in that room where we were both uneasy guests the way they had always touched. Instead it was as if the life we might have lived together had become the life we had really lived, and we were looking at each other across a place filled with houses we had lived in together and babies we had borne and love we had made, fights we had fought. There was no need to ask each other any more questions or to explain anything to each other because for the moment there was nothing about either of us we didn't know and hadn't always known.

She said, "I never told anybody," and I knew what she meant just as she'd known I'd know, meant she'd never told anybody how during that same sad time when Sharon and I had split up, I had asked myself to her house for supper once because I was bored and lonesome and though we didn't have much in common, we at least had Sir Peter Barrie and Ethan Frome and King Lear in common and I was at the point where I would have settled for a lot less. So I'd gone there at the appointed time not knowing that her mother was away and not remembering what a fatal mistake it always is for teacher and taught to try renewing old ties that work well enough in the classroom but vanish like smoke three weeks let alone five years or whatever after the last bell has rung on the last class. So the evening was a tongue-tied disaster for both of us, and I drank three desperate scotches to her one while we waited for supper to cook and one conversation ran out of gas after another until finally under the pretext of needing the can I beat it upstairs and wandered around up there until after a while she came up to see if I'd let myself out the window on a knotted sheet. It was then that in the First Communion hush of her bedroom between sheets blue with dusk we ended up making love together not all that less awkwardly than downstairs we had made conversation together but with the difference that from the little death of that second failure, a life branched off deep inside me which was no less alive for my having not only never actually, year-in-year-out, lived it but not even thought about it all that much, the way things go. A few months later when Laura married my nephew, I suppose we both must have thought about it separately, she and I, but at different moments and in different ways so that it was only that evening in Sutton when Tony and Sharon were putting the kids to bed and the pipes were thumping over our heads that we both thought about it together and it came alive for both of us at once.

A dying man's whole life passes in seconds before his eyes, they say, and to the extent that the whole life I might have lived with Laura passed then before mine, I suppose in a way I was dying myself. I felt the whole life I lived in that house with my real wife and real children shudder under me like an earthquake, and since the other life was not substantial enough to bear my weight either, for a moment it was as if an abyss had opened beneath me. I didn't even trust myself to speak for fear of what it could pitch me headlong into, so I might be sitting there still with cobwebs in my hair and my mouth full of silence if my son Bill hadn't come to the rescue. He piped word down that he wanted Laura and me to come kiss him goodnight so all I ever got around to

49

saying to her before we went on up was "Dear Brutus," I think, "Dear Brutus, dear Brutus"—breathing it more than saying it out where I could be sure that she'd heard it—but even that was enough to tremble its foundations again, the house that Jack built, before we reached the security of the second floor.

Sharon and Tony and Laura and I—I remember the four of us standing there around the bed where my skinny son lay so sleepy he was drunk, so drunk he hardly knew it when one after the other we kissed him, strange deputation that we were. Sharon and I were to be on our way before he was up the next morning so our goodnight was really our goodbye too although he was in no state at that point to know it or care much, and I wasn't either as I look back on it. When I whispered goodbye into his small, sweaty ear, I didn't let myself mean any more than just goodnight by it. Goodbye, goodbye. If you really stopped to think about it, I don't suppose you would ever say it.

CHAPTER FOUR

MY CHIEF TROUBLE with Callaway was that most of the time I had no clear idea what he was talking about. If I stopped to puzzle it out word by word, like bad handwriting, I was lost. The most I could hope for was the general drift, and even then I got it wrong as often as not. To cut short both my frustration and his, I would sometimes finish off what I thought was going to be his sentence only to find him swatting the air between us with his shapely black hand as if a bee was attacking him. What stung him, of course, was not my failure but his own. He knew he wasn't getting through and his desperate eyes told me he knew, his black face glowing with the misery of it like a coal. The misery made him talk even faster than he was talking already, the heavy, sweet Southern syllables getting all gummed together in odd clusters at that breakneck Northern speed. *Mustapha zigzag compustuck silo,* he would say. Something like that. Gertrude Conover claimed that over the years she had learned to understand him, but I had my doubts. She would tell me what he had said, either a verbatim translation or a loose paraphrase, but even when he bobbed his head around in endorsement, I suspected that it was less because she had rendered him right than that he admired her version for some special quality of its own.

"Whimsal ah humbleseep duggasick toe moe juffle," he said on the steps of the Lincoln Memorial with the sun blinding bright on the marble and a stiff breeze ballooning Sharon's skirt.

He said, "Tie mudruss begga dandyfay roesah." He was frowning up toward the rotunda where you could just make out the great figure enthroned in shadows. "Summa sot," he added in another voice, quieter, as if it might be a melancholy footnote to the rest. Summer's hot? Somersault? Gertrude Conover's hairnet had come loose in the breeze, and she had reached one lizard green arm across her face to fasten it. From under her arm she said, "When he was the Pharaoh, he had temples many times the size of this one, though some were not." The repairs completed, she lowered her arm to find the hairnet dangling from her bracelet. She yanked it loose and slipped it into her purse. "That's enough out of you," she said.

Callaway was standing several steps above us in black

trousers, shiny black shoes, a dazzling white shirt open at the collar and a green Agway cap with a visor. I wondered whether she had made the observation on her own or had been quoting him and, if quoting him, whether she had quoted him right. Did Callaway know of his former glory, remember temples he had presided over that made the Lincoln Memorial look like two cents?

When he turned around to gaze back across the Mall over our heads, his bony face under the visor looked like a black keyhole.

It was Gertrude Conover who had insisted on seeing the sights in Washington on our way south. Somewhere in Maryland with Callaway at the wheel and Sharon and me on either side of her in the back seat, she said, "No wonder it's taking me so long to work my way to cosmic consciousness. There are so many places I've never been, so many things I've never done, so many fascinating people I've never met. I simply can never resist another rebirth, even though I know perfectly well where it will get me in the end and where it won't get me, too. It's like eating salted peanuts. The more lives you live, the more lives you crave. I'm afraid I'm the eternal sightseer."

"Why not?" Sharon said. "You always seem to get the red carpet treatment. Back when you knew Bip in ancient Egypt you were a princess, you told him."

Gertrude Conover said, "Technically no. My father was only a Nubian tough who had the bad luck to get himself killed in a border free-for-all. It's true the Pharaoh took a shine to me and made me his ward, but properly speaking I was not a princess of the blood."

"Six of one," Sharon said.

I said, "In the eighteenth century you said you were an Italian contessa."

Gertrude Conover said, "I've never seen a century drag the way that one did. There were times I thought it would go on forever.

"But yes," she said. "I've always tried to keep my karma in good repair, and of course the pay-off has been that more often than not I've been born with a silver spoon in my mouth. Though not always, of course. When the Aryans were spreading out all over creation with their bad teeth and their impossible language, I starved to death in the Punjab, and at the time of the Viking raids on the English coast, I was witness to barbarities that would make your flesh crawl. Generally speaking, though, I don't deny what you've said, my dear. By and large I've traveled through history first class."

"Do you remember all those lives?" Sharon said.

Gertrude Conover said, "That's like when people ask me if I've read all the books in the library at Revonoc. I say what on earth would I want to do a thing like that for?"

I said, "In the ones you remember, did Bebb always turn up?"

"I always hoped he would," she said.

She was gazing out the car window as we talked, her face turned away from me, but I could see her eyes reflected in the glass, and beyond them, through them, the landscape racing by like the centuries.

She said, "You forget so much between lives—of course it would be unthinkable any other way. Just imagine remembering a thousand first loves, a thousand sets of children you bore and raised, a thousand wars. But Bebb I never forgot. In every new life I lived, there would come a moment when I remembered him. Something would happen to remind me or maybe I would catch sight of him waiting for me on the fringes of some dream I was dreaming. And then I would hope like anything that our paths would cross again. Sometimes they did, sometimes they didn't. And when they did, I won't say that it was all moonlight and roses, but one way or another, every time Bebb turned up, he made it a red-letter life."

She said, "It was his not turning up that made the eighteenth century such a flop—just one baby after another for years, not to mention the awful damp and people throwing their slops right into the public street."

I said, "Bebb must be an eternal sightseer too."

It made a good picture, I thought—the two of them touring through the ages together, meeting, parting, meeting again. She would know him by the way he sacrificed his unblemished lamb or shouldered his flintlock or blinked that trick eye of his under the velvet cap of some Renaissance shyster.

"Not Leo Bebb," she said. "You remember the summer we were all in England together, how restless he was—always in such a hurry to move on to the next place? It was never the sights that kept him moving—he hardly noticed them—and it has never been the sights that have kept him returning to this earth so many times either."

"How come he keeps doing it then?" Sharon asked.

Gertrude Conover said, "It is the nature of the man."

She said, "As long as there's anybody left to return to down here, Leo Bebb will always return to them. Return *for* them might be a better way of putting it."

She pulled a tourist map of Washington out of her purse and unfolded it across her knees. She said, "Leo Bebb is an always-returner, and that is the long and the short of it."

Once we arrived in Washington, something happened which made me believe for a time either that he had returned yet again or that as far as this particular life was concerned, he had never left in the first place. Our tour of historic landmarks had taken us to the Library of Congress where we drifted off into different sections of a large exhibition room, and I was wandering around only half seeing the things they had set out in the glass cases. I remember a matching set of white beads and white earrings that Mary Lincoln had apparently been partial to and a photograph of Harry Truman standing under a rack of neckties in the days he ran a haberdashery. I remember thinking how if you didn't happen to know about all the sleaziness and double-dealing that have gone on in Washington over the years, you might never guess it from the kind of shabby, sad things it chooses to treasure or from the look of the stately, hopeful Federal buildings with their soaring columns and Justice, Liberty, Truth, all the great abstractions, carved into their facades like New Year's resolutions before the hangover sets in. It is a very touching, very vulnerable city to me, and I can never return to it without feeling a lump in the throat. It affects me like that scene in *Ruggles of Red*

Gap where Charles Laughton recites the Gettysburg Address in the saloon and the faces of the crowd go still and soft at the sound of it and the faces of the audience watching it thirty years later go stiller and softer yet at the sense of a time gone by when the Gettysburg Address could mean so much. In other words I was thinking wistful thoughts as I drifted through that place, and in that sense I suppose you could say I was ready for what happened next although in every other sense I was not ready at all.

What happened next was that I noticed a staircase that led up not to another floor as far as I could tell but to a closed door set into the wall, and it seemed such an odd thing for a staircase to do that I decided to go take a look. My guess was that the door would turn out to lead to an office of some sort or another room full of memorabilia, but I was wrong. Stepping through the door, I found myself standing on a balcony looking down into the rotunda of the main reading room below.

It was an enormous, lamp-lit cavern of a place with its ornate marble walls, arches, balustrades, and soaring skylit dome, its mighty circulation desk and curved ranks of file drawers with a card each for all the books ever published in the universe. Except for a vague rustling sound, people dwarfed by the balcony's height moved noiselessly across acres of floor or sat at long tables lost in their reading. It was the living heart of the library that I'd stumbled on, and I had the sense of great pulse and purpose, of librarians with their hair in buns telling the Dewey decimal system like beads, of the unscuffed soles of statesmen heavy on the thick carpet, of congressmen and scholars grave and quiet as carp in the depths of their concentration. Then I thought I saw Bebb.

I saw a shiny pink scalp set atop a pair of thick shoulders anyway. I saw a plump hand turn a page. On an empty chair beside him I saw what looked like a black raincoat and a Tyrolean hat. And then as suddenly as I'd seen him, I lost him again.

A woman in a green dress holding a child by the hand moved between us; there was a shifting of positions; for an instant a shape blotted out the light of the reading lamp, then withdrew again, and in the dazzle of it I saw that Bebb was gone. Unless a figure I could only partly see crouched at a lower drawer of the card catalogue was Bebb. I leaned out as far as I dared to see if it was but couldn't. I would have shouted down to him if the great size and hush of the place hadn't stopped my mouth, would have jumped down to him if it had been twenty feet instead of what seemed a hundred. It was only when I saw him that I realized it was the sight I'd longed for above all others.

Dear Bebb. What was there about him? It is hard to say exactly. He never had that much time for me, not even when he must have known I most needed him. He was always in a hurry, always so intent on the next thing he had to do, as Gertrude Conover pointed out in the car, that you felt he wasn't entirely with you even when he was. He was by no means the wisest person I've ever known or the most eloquent or the most warm-hearted and heaven knows he had his shadow side like the rest of us. Not even counting his five years in the pen, or his smog-bound finances, or the ambiguous nature of his various evangelical enterprises, you had the feeling that during his life and for all I know during innumerable

58

other lives thrown in he had moved through dark and painful places that had left that one gimpy eye of his needing to flutter closed every once in a while to shut out the dark and painful memory of them. And yet, what was there about him that made me miss him more than any man? Even at his lowest and bluest, there was a life in him that rubbed off on you, that's all. You might feel better or you might feel worse when Bebb was around, but in any case you felt more. There was more of you to feel with.

So there in the Library of Congress I was prepared to do almost anything. If Bebb was down there, I had to get to him. There was somebody crouching half out of sight who might be Bebb, and if it was, he might have seen me, might be looking up surreptitiously at me even as I stood there looking down at him. He might not want to give himself away to me for fear that in my excitement I might give him away to God knows who, so I tried signaling to him in a way that I thought would catch nobody's eye that wasn't on me already, tried wagging my hand back and forth at chest level and then pointing down into the reading room to show him I'd be down there myself in no time flat and to wait.

As I rushed back through the exhibition room, I noticed Sharon and Gertrude Conover off looking at things in a corner, but I not only didn't have time to tell them what I was up to, something in me didn't even want to tell them. For fear they'd think I'd gone off my rocker maybe, or maybe, beneath that, the fear they'd come along and somehow dim for me a moment that all my life I'd been waiting for without knowing I was waiting for it.

I clattered down a flight of marble steps, two at a time, raced through corridors, and finally found myself at a pair of swinging leather doors which I pushed my way through to find that I was in the great reading room at last.

It took me a few moments to get oriented. I spotted my balcony, the circulation desk. The woman in the green dress was standing at it listening to a man with spectacles pushed back on his forehead telling her something soundlessly. Beyond her was the table where Bebb had been reading, if it was Bebb, or pretending to read, if he was pretending. Beyond that were the curved ranks of the card catalogue. I made a rapid tour through all of them, but there was no longer anyone crouched at the lower drawers, and I recognized nobody. My heart leapt when from behind I saw a bald man reaching for a volume of the Cumulative Book Index, but when I positioned myself to see his face, it was comprehensively not Bebb's—a flabby, tired face with a small pink moustache.

The woman with the green dress had seated herself at one of the long tables and was filling out some kind of form while beside her the child, a boy about eight, was goggling up at the sky-light fathoms above us in the dome. I went up to the woman and explained my problem. From a distance I thought I had recognized an old friend sitting near her. Did she by any chance remember a stout man with a bald head, sixtyish, clean-shaven I was about to add but didn't then. For all I knew he'd grown a beard. For all I knew he'd grown another face. Did an always-returner always return looking the same?

"You notice anybody looked like that, honey?" the

woman said to the little boy.

The boy said, "There was a man that winked his eye at me," and again my heart leapt.

"A bald man?" I asked.

"He had a hat on."

"You remember what kind of a hat?"

"Just a plain hat."

"Fat?"

"Hat," he said. "He had on a hat, and he winked at me."

I said, "You didn't happen to notice where he went, did you?"

He pointed at the sky light. "Up there's the tallest window in the whole world."

"You don't happen to see him anywhere in this room still, I suppose."

"I seen his eye wink," the boy said. "He winked like this." He screwed up one whole side of his face to get the eye closed.

I thanked them for their help.

I didn't tell Sharon and Gertrude Conover what had happened because I wasn't sure if anything had happened. Gertrude Conover was buying postcards, and Sharon was sitting on a radiator with one bare foot in her hand. I asked her where Callaway was.

"He went to the can," she said. "He seemed like he was in a real hurry."

I said, "He wasn't having one of his nosebleeds was he?" At the thought of that telltale nose of Callaway's, my heart leapt a third time.

She said, "I didn't ask him what he was going to do in there."

Gertrude Conover appeared with her postcards fanned out like a bridge hand. She said, "The Folger Shakespeare Library is only a skip and a jump away. It's the largest collection of first folios in existence."

Sharon said, "Gertrude Conover, did you ever run into Shakespeare in one of your other lives?" She was leaning forward to fold her toes back and forth, and her hair covered half her face.

Gertrude Conover said, "My dear, Shakespeare was a nobody. He pronounced his r's like w's and couldn't even spell his own name properly."

"No shit," Sharon said. She seemed genuinely interested.

When Callaway reappeared, I asked him if his nose had been giving him trouble. He seemed to find my question amusing and smiled broadly. "Joppa dill," he said. Then, taking his handkerchief out of his pocket and holding it balled up to his nose, he said, "Possum," and laughed.

Since Gertrude Conover had already headed out through the revolving door for the Folger, she was not there to interpret for me.

CHAPTER FIVE

SHARON SAID, "No wonder Bebb hightailed out of here first chance he got. Jesus."

Poinsett, South Carolina, was less a town than an intersection. There was a dry cleaner, a package store, a quonset hut converted into a v.f.w. headquarters. The post office, we eventually discovered, was in a store that sold groceries, drugs, drygoods, sex magazines, and personalized compacts with names like Earlene and Cindi and Kimberly on them. Over the cash register was the first strip of flypaper I'd seen in years, all gummed up with flies that looked as though they might have landed there during the Hoover administration. There were two big gas stations with plastic pennants and revolving signs. There was a Baptist Church with a triangle of dead grass in front of it and a bulletin board that read "Redemption Center—no green stamps required." A railroad track cut across the road we entered on, and we had to wait for an endless freight train to pass by. Callaway counted the cars while we waited, and when the caboose rolled by, he said "Sixty-two" so loud and clear that for once I understood him perfectly. Between the two gas stations there was a Chicken in the Basket place made of white tile like a men's room, and even with the windows of Gertrude Conover's Lincoln closed tight and the airconditioning on high, we could smell the smell of frying fat. It must have been ninety in the shade, if there had been any shade instead of just miles of flat red farmland, peach orchards, a trailer park. Off toward the horizon was a hazy stack of buildings that was Spartanburg.

I tried to picture Bebb there fifty years earlier, tried to remember what little he'd told me about his life there. He'd said his father was a house painter who'd been crippled by a fall and spent most of the rest of his life in bed. He'd spoken of a hard-working mother who had managed to keep the family going and had been the one who started him off on the sawdust trail. Somehow he conveyed the impression to me that she herself had never followed it far enough beyond faith to make it to charity but had bogged down somewhere just short of hope. I remembered his describing one time as a child when he'd found a crated coffin awaiting shipment on the railroad platform and had seen as clearly as if it had been made of glass an old woman stretched out inside it with a pair of pink bloomers on and a piece of sticking

64

plaster over her mouth. He'd told me of seeing piles of peaches rotting by the side of the road where they'd been dumped to keep the price up when there were people who couldn't afford the price of a peach. He said it was what sin was all about. The first job he'd had was washing dishes at a restaurant in Spartanburg where he had wooed and won the boss's daughter Lucille Yancey. From there he had gone on to selling Bibles. The only building I could see that looked as if it might have been standing in those days was the grocery store–post office where we went to ask the whereabouts of the old Bebb place.

I marvel at the figure we must have cut as we filed in—Gertrude Conover in her blue hair and white shoes, dressed for cocktails on the terrace at Revonoc; Sharon with dark glasses the size of butter-plates, bellbottoms, and her shirttails knotted in front to keep her midriff bare; Callaway looking more like a chauffeur than usual except for his Agway cap. A bell over the screen door announced our arrival but it might as well have saved itself the trouble. Everybody looked our way as the man behind the post office grille repeated our phrase back at us a few times—old Bebb place, old Bebb place—sweeping his eye around the store to make sure nobody was missing anything. Nobody was. There were a couple of youths thumbing through the magazines, a girl with a bad complexion waiting on an old man in the grocery department, a few others. The postmaster was all Adam's apple and teeth as he leaned his forehead against the bars.

It had never occurred to me to work out a strategy, but under his gaze I found myself not wanting to go into details. I didn't want to tell him any more than I had to about why we were there and what we were after—

partly, I suppose, because when you got right down to it, we weren't all that sure ourselves what we were after any more than Bebb had been sure, saying just to do something nice for Jesus down there, whatever that meant, whoever Jesus was. Gertrude Conover said, "We were motoring by and just thought we'd like to see where a dear old friend was born. Well, it is a kind of sentimental journey," and I felt that like me she was reluctant to say who the dear old friend was as though at the sound of his name they might all rend their garments and the crops would fail. As a result the man rambled on about Bebbs in Greenville, Saluda, Tryon, speaking in one of those Southern accents that's less of a drawl than a sly little pussyfoot patter up near the front of the mouth, and I found myself not wanting to cut him short for fear of putting him in some queer way on guard. I felt he was looking at us queerly enough as it was and remembered all the movies I'd ever seen about Yankees getting locked up in just such a Dixie backwash as this for conduct no more suspicious. I thought I could see him wince inwardly at the free and comradely way Sharon rested her arm on Callaway's shoulder as she leaned over to take off one shoe.

Then it was Sharon who finally came out with it. She said, "Anybody here know a place where a man use to live by the name of *Leo* Bebb?" and the old man buying groceries set his bag down on the counter as if he could handle only one thing at a time and said, "Leo Bebb, he used to buy scratch off me back when I had the feed store. He'd come say Sam, let me have a hundred, didn't say a hundred this or that. Seemed like he was always in a hurry, couldn't only say but a hundred, Sam. Course I knew it was scratch. Always *was* scratch," which wasn't much in the way of a souvenir and yet "Ah did you once see Shelley plain," I thought, "and did he stop and speak to you?" those same watery old eyes goggling out at a Bebb unimaginably young and untouched but even then in a hurry. The man behind the bars finally got around to saying there was only one Bebb place he knew in Poinsett—he pronounced it Points—and showed us how to get there on Callaway's map. Babe's place, he said. Babe Bebb? He didn't seem to want to go into details either. Back in the car again Gertrude Conover said, "There was something about that old man having known him. He put his thumb right on my heart."

It wasn't the place of our dreams when we got to it, at least not of my dreams—no silvery clapboard, sway-back roof and forlorn, abandoned windows, no waist-high grass at the busted porch steps. There was nothing Andrew Wyeth about it, just a big, square two-story house like a child's drawing of a house. It had black asbestos shingles with a white trim and was set not far off the red clay road. The grass out front was mowed to within an inch of its life and by the front door there was a tractor tire painted white with nasturtiums in it. There was a birdbath supposed to look like antique stone, a Chipmunk Crossing sign and two plastic flamingos, one looking skyward, one pecking for something to eat in the scorched grass. By the side door stood a couple of gas cylinders screened behind white palings and nailed to the palings a sign that read:

"Looks like there's Bebbs here all right," Sharon said. Nobody answered the bell if it even worked, but the door was open and we went in.

The Uforium. Just inside the door you ran into a partition blocking your way with a rainbow-colored painting of a flying saucer on it. The saucer had a low crown and a wide brim like a cardinal's hat, and it was tilted toward the earth at a rakish angle as if the cardinal might have had one too many. The door in the crown was flung wide, and out of it a comic strip balloon streamed up into the toy-blue sky with the message *"Hurry Aboard! It's later than you think!"* lettered on it. On a table in front of it was a contribution box, a book to sign, and a glass with some of the nasturtiums in it. Behind the partition was the Uforium proper.

It was the light that struck you first, a yellowish, extraterrestrial glow that came through the fly-specked window shades that were all pulled down to the bottom. There were pictures of flying saucers on the walls, photographs mostly, some with portholes, some spoked like wagon wheels, some just streaks of light on the horizon or dots in the sky that an amateur might have mistaken for birds. There were pictures of people who had seen flying saucers and pictures that these people had evidently made of what they had seen. One of them showed a figure with a head like a radio tube and one big eye where his navel should have been. Around the room under the windows there were exhibition cases with glass lids, and in one of them there was an enlarged Kodacolor close-up of a human mouth. Next to it in the case were some small pellets that looked like mouse droppings. The mouth was wide open so you could see the teeth, and on the crown of each tooth was a dark spot that looked like one of the mouse droppings. Sharon said, "Hey Bopper, want to see some outer space cow-flops?"—some flat, roughly circular objects about the size of dinner plates. They seemed to be plaster casts of something.

In the center of the room on a large, low table like the kind F.A.O. Schwarz used to display electric trains on at Christmas time there was a relief map painted psyche-delic green with different colored pins stuck in here and there all over it—yellow pins for landings, a card ex-plained, red ones for sightings, blue ones for hearings. On a sloping hillside there was a question mark made up out of pins of all three colors. Around the edge of the table were burned places where people had apparently left their cigarettes and forgotten them. Sharon came over and breathed something in my ear. She said, "I've just had a sighting," and pointed to the far end of the room where there was a door standing ajar. Through the door you could see part of a window and part of a table. On the table you could see part of a human being. It was a hand. As I approached, I saw a puff of smoke drift down towards it.

The hand belonged to a fat woman who seemed long since to have forgotten it. She was sitting there gazing out the window with her back to me, a flyswatter on the table beside her. She had bare, fleshy arms and a pink ribbon tied in her grey curls. Except for the tangle of cigarette smoke, there was such stillness about her that she could have been part of the Uforium, the waxwork of a flying saucer captain's wife watching the sky for saucers. There wasn't much for her to see through the window, just the stretch of red clay road we'd come on and our car parked out front with Callaway drowsing behind the wheel. I had to speak twice before she turned around.

I remember still the way she looked that first time I ever laid eyes on her, before I even knew her name—that plaintive, fat face as she bit the inside of her lip crooked, her forehead dimpling like a child's desperate to go to the john but scared to ask, those eyebrows she'd tried to pencil on where she didn't have any eyebrows of her own. You could see the thick grey curls were a wig. She didn't have a real hair on her head. Her cigarette was in her mouth and one eye squinnied up against the smoke, her small features huddled together as if for protection behind it. Was she Mrs. Bebb, I asked. Was she Mrs. Bebb? Twice. I had the impression that she wasn't answering right off the bat because for a moment, come upon suddenly that way, she wasn't sure. I had the impulse to take the cigarette out from between her lips for her the way they do in the movies for dying soldiers, but she managed with it still in place finally, talking around it like a thumb. Whispering almost. I still remember too the first time I heard that breathy little babydoll voice she had that turned everything she said into a tiny question she sounded afraid there was no answer to. "I'm Bertha Bebb?" she said. "Babe's downstreet?" then that hand that still didn't seem to belong to her bringing the swatter down hard on a fly on the window sill. The working end of the swatter was baby-blue like a rattle.

I could see her face register the appearance of Gertrude Conover, who came edging into the doorway beside me, her voice coming out under my armpit like an inaugural address compared to Bertha Bebb's. She said, "We're looking for an old house that hasn't been lived in for years. You've had your Uforium here long?" Hearing it spoken for the first time, I heard it *euphorium*.

Bertha Bebb said, "Want to see the moonrocks till Babe comes?" When she got up out of her chair I saw she was wearing men's shoes and bobby socks, passing through the door as vague and shapeless as weather. She carried the swatter in one hand and the cigarette in the other. She didn't look at Sharon as she passed, just said "Hey" to her. Sharon said, "Hey." Bertha Bebb said, "Here's the *moonrocks?* Don't touch them barehanded. They're all over moongerms?" She poked at them with the swatter, her forehead still puckering in hectic, worried ways. The moonrocks looked like bits of broken cinderblock.

"I thought all the moonrocks were in places like Washington, D.C.," Sharon said. "Where'd you get these moonrocks from?"

"From the moon?" she said. She said, "Every step you take you bounce higher than a kite. Babe says he broke wind once? He was twenty minutes walking back to where he took off."

Sharon said, "Bip would have gotten a bang out of that one," getting a bang out of it herself, that sudden flash of guilty smile. Bertha Bebb wasn't getting a bang out of it, looking afraid she'd said something wrong.

"Luce always said Bip was from outer space himself," Sharon said, and there had been times I almost believed she was right. Bebb in a beanie Sharon had given him in Florida once with two little pinwheels over the ears spinning wildly as we sped home from Lion Country in his open car. Bebb in a Lexington Avenue Chock Full O'Nuts where the man behind the counter had a silvery, ageless face and silvery hair and Bebb said you got two kinds from outer space, silvers and goldens, and this one was a silver. Lucille said it took one to know one.

I heard Gertrude Conover saying, "Has your husband been to the moon, Mrs. Bebb?" Been to Cincinnati, been to the barber's. The fathomless imperturbability of Gertrude Conover, I thought. For all I knew she had been to the moon herself some other life or so.

Bertha Bebb raised a glass lid and took out something that looked like a badly charred pair of football shoulderpads. She said, "It's all there's left of his *space* suit? It burnt the minute the air hit it."

"Oh dear, what a shame," Gertrude Conover said, running her fingers down one dangling strap. "I hope he wasn't wearing it at the time."

Bertha Bebb said, "The air's different up there. There's more room in it? Babe saw a pack of them bigger than him in a space he couldn't hardly squeeze into, his ownself, here on earth."

"What's a hearing?" Sharon said.

Bertha Bebb took a puff on her cigarette, letting the smoke come out helter-skelter with her words. She said, "There's one," using her swatter to tap the case with the open mouth and the mouse droppings in it.

Sharon said, "You hear with your *mouth?*"

Bertha Bebb said, "Not my mouth."

Despite the earlier warning, Gertrude Conover had picked up a moonrock, but I noticed that she had slipped on one of her white gloves first. She said, "There are some that you hear then, and there are some that you see . . ." She waved the moonrock toward the photographs on the wall. "Tell us about the ones that actually land, Mrs. Bebb."

Bertha Bebb said, "The horses go crazy sometimes, near to kick the stalls out." It was the most positive she'd sounded yet, as though at least about the horses there was no room for doubt. She said, "Sometimes they climb right out and poke into things? They've been doing it since Bible times."

"Bip always said they were the same as the angels," Sharon said.

"Silvers and goldens," I said. "He said goldens were scarce as hen's teeth."

"Don't hold your breath till you see your next silver either," Sharon said.

Bertha Bebb said, "Babe's been aboard? They gave him things? He'll show you some if you have a consultation."

Gertrude Conover put the moonrock back where it belonged and peeled off her glove. She looked quite young in the smoky, yellow light. She said, "Well you see it's not a consultation we came for. We just hoped he could help us locate the place we're looking for."

Bertha Bebb said, "He helps anybody he can lay his hands on?"

There was a sound of raindrops on the roof, the first

unevenly spaced drops of a rain just starting, and then Sharon said, "Was there ever anybody lived in this place years ago by the name of Leo Bebb?" Letting the suspicion drift out as easy as the name: that these Bebbs were squatters, that beneath the black asbestos shingles and white trim was the weathered clapboard of my dreams, this very room the room Bebb had come back to the sadder and the wiser from the old lady with sticking plaster on her mouth at the Spartanburg depot.

Sharon stood on one side of the map and Bertha Bebb on the other, and I remember thinking there should have been a new pin stuck somewhere into the hills between them to mark the hearing that took place then as the name of Leo Bebb was spoken and heard.

"Has he passed?" Bertha Bebb said as soft as the sound on the roof, *passed* in the sense of passing by, passing through, I thought, until Sharon said, "A year ago this spring."

Bertha Bebb was still holding the charred shoulder-pads, and she went to put them back. From the way she lowered the glass lid over them with her fat shoulders humped forward, her grey curls shaking, you would have thought it was made of lead. Her back was turned. After a while, she said, "You kin?"

A whiff of wet came wafting into the Uforium. A fly buzzed three circles above us before landing on a lamp by the door.

"He was my daddy," Sharon said.

Bertha Bebb turned around, pushing the smoke aside like a curtain. She said, "Lucille's baby?"

Sharon shook her head. "Bip adopted me."

Bertha Bebb's voice was so quiet now I couldn't hear

74

what she said, but Sharon heard.

"It's Sharon," she said.

Bertha Bebb said something else.

"If he knew, he never told me," Sharon said.

Then after a long pause, the quietest thing of all from Bertha Bebb. I don't think anybody heard it, not even Sharon, but from the way she stood there with the smoke sliding up her fat wrist you could tell that it was a question and that it had to be answered, so for lack of anybody else I answered it. I said, "Leo Bebb," then just stood there and watched the landing the name made, soft as rain, on that great moon of a face.

She noticed the fly on the lamp eventually and let him have it with her baby-blue swatter. It was a glass lamp that broke in two when it hit the linoleum. The fly escaped unharmed.

CHAPTER SIX

SHARON SAID, "You look enough like him to be his twin brother. My God."

Babe said, "Honey, I am his twin brother."

Sharon said, "I never heard him tell he had any twin brother."

Babe said, "Child, you ever try making a list of all the things you never heard your daddy tell? You ever try catching a summer breeze in a bag?"

Sharon said, "You had the same mother and daddy and you were raised on the same place?"

"Rat," Babe said.

"This same house?"

76

"Rat," Babe said.

To his wife he said, "Don't you mind about this, hear." The broken lamp dangled from his hand by its cord, head down like a dead chicken. With his arm around her shoulder he gave her a squeeze that undimpled her forehead, her small features unhuddling enough to let a smile slip through. Her step was light as a girl's as she left, the grey curls bouncing. "That's my Shirley Temple, my own sweet love," he said.

Only then, starting with Sharon and clutching out from her, did he manage to scramble his arms around all three of us at once in a great football huddle embrace smelling of plastic and rain, his words coming out half muffled, "Oh I knew you were coming. I knew you quick as a wink." When he took his arms away, we came apart like a barrel.

Except for his damp red hair all clumped and ragged like something chewed by a goat, he could have been Bebb if you didn't look too hard—Bebb in a fright wig, Bebb having gained a few pounds and aged a few years. He had less the look of Bebb's hard-rubber bounce to him than of something with give to it, comfier, his plump Bebbsian face a New Year's Eve balloon on New Year's Day, but bug-eyed and jazzy like Bebb with no neck to speak of, a tight-lipped Kewpie-doll H of a mouth. There was a lot more cracker in his voice. His *right* came through *rat*, his *I* the sound you make around a tongue depressor when they tell you to open up wider and try again, but his mouth snapped open and shut on his words like a trap the same way, the same scrubbed look of a fat nun. It was like seeing somebody in a dream who's died and you're so glad to see him again that you can hardly stand it, yet all the time you know deep down that it isn't really who you think it is because there's some emptiness inside that the sight of him doesn't fill the way food doesn't fill you in dreams either. It was almost but not quite Bebb there, Babe instead with his spikes of rainy red hair and his see-through plastic raincoat that you could see his sleazy slacks through, his rolled up shirtsleeves, his pot swelling out over his belt in a way Bebb's never would have. Bebb was always too buttoned in, trussed up for that, almost always. Babe didn't seem in a hurry like Bebb, seemed looser, pinker. And there was nothing wrong with either of his eyes. I kept watching for a telltale flutter. There was nothing.

To Sharon he said, "Child, your daddy and me we sprouted up from seeds in the same womb. The first thing I ever touched was your daddy tucked up next me in the same dark. First thing I ever heard was him holler out when they whumped the breath of life into him five minutes after they left off whumping me. It wasn't just the same milk we drunk out of the same teats, it was all the same first sights and smells and sounds of life. You take a pair of chimps humped up together in a cage with their big scared eyes watching out through the bars, that was your daddy and me to a T. Watching the sky turn black as thunder. Watching our cripple daddy staring out the window at us with his unshaved whiskers. Watching the fearsome things shadows do on the ceiling nights if somebody bumps the bulb and hearing our poor, wore-out mama say bitter words made her wish she'd bit her tongue out soon as she said them. We were a pair of comical-looking little fat chimps hanging on to each other for dear life while the world come bearing down on us like a express train." A flying saucer hovered above him like a hat and above that the sounds of Bertha moving around upstairs looking for flies.

Sharon said, "Bip never talked about it. I couldn't ever picture him being any different than the way I knew him, and all the time I knew him he looked the same. Luce said she bet even in his crib he used to lay there fat and bald-headed in his double-breasted suit."

Babe said, "The only toy we had between us was a beat-up old Erector set with a wind-up motor they give us out of the missionary box because they were ashamed to ship it off that way to the heathen. It use to set over there under the moonrocks. Daddy use to lay on a sofa next the stove. If the hens weren't setting right, Mother she'd bring and lay eggs up around him where the warmth would hatch them out. Didn't he use to cackle his head off just to spite her when the Eastern Stars come," and then "Bawk, bawk, bawk, *begawk*," Babe went with his head rocked back like a man gargling, "puck, puck, puck, *petawket*," with tears of amusement welling up in his eyes. "Laugh? I . . ."

"No wonder Bip never made a feature of talking about it," Sharon said. She traced a raindrop down the wavy pane behind her.

He said, "Honey, he just turned the lock on those times and threw out the key. He was a bag stuffed full of times he didn't talk about. He made out like the only time it ever was was the present time and you better make the most of that before it got stuffed in the bag too. He cleared out of Points first chance he got because Points was those two little sadsack chimps with a setting hen for a father and a bitter blow for a mother plus a few other things besides he'd stuffed away and sat on the lid on. Now I stayed put. Maybe I just didn't have the get up and go. I didn't try to make out like things never happened that happened. Maybe I should of. I moved right in on those things. I took over this pitiful place all stunk up with the old days like they were something crawled in between the walls and died, and I moved the future in like furniture. What you're looking at it's the future," he said, including the whole Uforium with the sweep of his arm.

"Friends," he said, "there's lots of kooks and phonies in this business, but what we've got here, it's treasure from on high. It's the hope of the world come true."

When he mentioned moving in and taking over, I thought the moment had come to bring up for better or worse the whole delicate business of what we were there for, but as soon as he started in on the Uforium, I decided that it would be like passing the plate during the elevation of the host.

Gertrude Conover said, "You said you were expecting us and you recognized us right away. Those seem very remarkable things, Mr. Bebb."

Babe said, "I've seen things and done things that make recognizing you folks look like a card trick."

"It's interesting you should say that," Gertrude Conover said, "because I believe in remarkable things myself. All my life I've hungered after them the way other people hunger after money or God. I am an old woman, but I have never given up the hope that before my time comes, I will see something truly remarkable. If your brother were here he would quote Scripture to me. My dear," she said, turning to Sharon, "what's the part about the man who saw Jesus as a baby and said now at last he could die happy?"

Babe waited while Sharon shook her head. Then he said, "Lord, now lettest thou thy servant depart in peace, for mine eyes have seen thy salvation, Gertrude Conover." He said both of her names together the way Bebb always had, and you could see that it had its effect on her as she stood there with the one white glove that she'd put on for protection against moongerms.

"I thought I had gotten over the worst part of missing him," she said. "You must miss him too."

Looking down at his wet shoes, his eyebrows raised, he said, "For forty years we didn't give each other as much as the time of day."

Later, when the show came, it came without warning. It had started to rain hard, and standing in the streaming doorway Gertrude Conover tried to signal Callaway to come in if he wanted to, but he didn't see her. Of all the things we were there to talk about we talked about none of them but the rain instead, the trip down, a place to stay nearby. Like a great wave, the discovery of Babe and who he was had carried us so far so fast that when it receded we were left high and dry, gasping for anything to say that would disguise what utter strangers we were. And then out of the blue he said, "Now you just watch this," and with a snap of his wrist sent something spinning through the air, then another and another until there were as many as three or four of them moving slowly through the air at once. Some landed on the relief map where he seemed to be aiming them, some clattered to the floor, slid off into corners. There was a whole drawer of them apparently—flat, round, colorless—and like an overfed discobolous he half crouched there in the dim light with his see-through raincoat touching the floor as he skimmed more and more of them out toward the map.

At the same time he must have thrown some switch because in addition to the flying saucers, the air was filled with flying saucer noises, the blips and beeps of electronic sound, insect-like chirpings. Lights came flashing off and on, little pinpoints of light, flotillas of them, spinning around the room with the saucers and saucer sounds until I began to lose all track of the fly-specked shades, the photographs, the rain, and it was as if Sharon and Gertrude Conover and I were floating through outer space ourselves. Like Romeo cut out in little stars so all the world would be in love with night, the strobes made constellations of us, the Blue Curls and Bare Midriff taking their place with the Big Dipper and Orion as there slowly floated to the surface of all the other sounds the sound of Babe's recorded voice sonorous and crepuscular like the travelogue narrator of my youth bidding his sunset farewells. "They're coming," he said, "just like we always dreamed they would. They're falling soft as goose down. They're twittering like birds in spring. The sky's ablaze, the heaven's afire."

"Old folks in nursing homes look up," Babe's voice said, "and folks in hospitals with tubes running through them and needles under their skin. Poor folks look up that can't afford shoes for their children's feet. The children look up—the little one with the harelip on him, the one her daddy twists her little arm off nearly when he comes home drunk and out of work. The whores with their painted lips and the sodomites look up. The rich folks with their treasure stored up where moth and rust doth corrupt and thieves break through and steal. And the thieves look up through the lonesome bars of their cage. Folks, we're all looking up at where hope comes from, and there's not a pair of eyes that isn't wet with tears."

Like a plague of locusts the cosmic chirpings grew in volume, then subsided again. Babe's recording said, "They're better than us up there. They're a zillion times smarter. Where we've got shots against measles and whooping cough, they've got shots against death. They don't war and raise hell with each other because they don't have to. They've each one got all they want and then some. They got us on their minds, friends. They're all heart, and they're set on bailing us out soon as ever they can. There's a few have paid us visits already. All we got to do is show them we're ready, and that's where SOS comes in.

"First there's S for signals. The wrong signal's worse than none. Find out how to signal from your own place right. That's how they know they got friends down here waiting.

"Next there's O for outerspace-watch. If we don't keep a watch on day and night, we'll never know when they're coming. Then too it's the way we know when one of them touches down for a look-see. Sign up for outer space watch.

"The last S is Saturday meeting. At Saturday meeting we get to find out who our friends are. We swap sightings. We listen to hearings. Folks, the most important part of Saturday meeting is we all get together just to plain *look up*.

"So that's SOS.

"Shove Off Soon.

"Send On Spacemen.

"Save Our Skins. Meantime if you've got a SOS needs attending to out of your own life, sign up to see Babe Bebb. Consultations by appointment only."

The canned speech, the beeps, the lights, they all ended as suddenly as they had begun, and into the fresh silence Sharon's voice fell small and flat as a coin. "Jesus," she said. "It's Bip all over with the Gospel left out."

With her loveliest souvenir of an eighteenth century smile Gertrude Conover said, "Lord now lettest thou thy servant depart in peace."

When Babe looked at me, I couldn't think of a thing to say. We'd run out of Dewar's and by now the package store would be closed up tight. We had no place to spend the night. I'd never been persuaded even by Bebb's eloquence that the Gospel was for me, but when it was left out, I missed it. The floor was littered with what I could see were some sort of plastic container lids. They said Sunshine on them. I had the kind of headache that clamps down tight like a football helmet. I forced some sort of ghastly smile, and even as I felt it turning to stone, Babe reached out with his plump hand and touched my cheek the way he might have reached out to straighten a picture. "Why you're all wore out, boy," he said. It would be impossible to overstate the effect of his diagnosis.

84

You put up a brave front in this world, especially if it's the world I was born into. No matter what sad thing happens, you go on with business as usual if for no other reason than that it would never do to let down in front of the help. You go on teaching your ninth graders the difference between *like* and *as*. You keep the lawn mowed in the summer and the walk shoveled in the winter. When you find out your wife has been cheating on you with your muscle-bound nephew, you don't throw them out but get out yourself. You move into Mrs. Gunther's boarding house where after a while things work themselves out somehow and you get back together again so almost entirely as if nothing had ever happened that it might as well not have, for all you take away from it that might have saved your soul. When at an odd, disconnected moment in your life you shack up with a girl like Laura Fleischman only to drift through it like a ghost, you don't either mourn your lost youth or make a wild stab at recapturing it. You just reconcile yourself to spending the rest of your middle age making the best of things because you can no longer make the most of them. When your father-in-law goes up in flames on a New Jersey potato field, there goes up with him what's probably the only chance you'll ever get to make a fool of yourself worth making.

With his smile shimmering like a moonlit ruin, Brownie tells you he's lost his faith.

Tony picks up what may or may not be your daughter Lucy and says, "Well I'll be goddammed."

"Why you're all wore out," Babe said, touching my face. He said, "Why you're all wore out, boy," and it was like hearing my name spoken in a place where I thought there was no one who knew it and I'd all but forgotten it myself.

When Callaway appeared at last, running through the rain with a piece of newspaper over his head, Babe moved us all on into the living room which turned out to look much as I imagined it must have in Bebb's day—a slippery horsehair sofa with an oval photograph over it of what might have been Bebb's grandparents standing shoulder to shoulder like a police line-up. They looked goiterish, overupholstered and mentally unsound. There was a parlor organ with pieces of worn carpet on the treadle, a plastic poinsettia plant, a wastepaper basket stuck all over with seashells. From where I sat the stairway was visible through the door and I could see the socks and shoes of Bertha Bebb sitting at the top of it. The very air smelled of the nineteenth century and there must have been things in there that hadn't been touched since nineteenth century fingers had touched them, and yet I remember thinking that for all I knew contacts of Babe's from outer space might have padded across those rag rugs, and looked at the same things I was looking at through whatever they used for eyes.

Bebb had left the house to Sharon, but Babe was living in it. Bebb had told us to do something nice for Jesus with it, but Babe was already doing something with it which, though maybe it wasn't just what Bebb had in mind, had at least a quality to it that he would have found not uncongenial. Even with the Gospel left out, there was lots of hope in it, and I felt sure Bebb would have liked the part about everybody looking up—the sodomites, the sick people with needles under their skins. So I think if I had had my way I would have simply let well enough alone and started heading for home as soon as we decently could. But not Sharon.

Sitting next to Babe on the horsehair sofa she told him the house he was living in was her house, and if she didn't say that she was planning to put him out on the street, she didn't say she wasn't either, but all of this in such an easy, loose-limbed kind of way, with whatever Southern accent she'd lost up North coming back as if she'd never lost it, that there was nothing Babe could have gotten hold of to hit her back with even if he'd felt like hitting her. Whatever came to matter to her later on, what mattered to her then, I think, was not that Bebb had left her a house but that he'd left her a past, a background, an origin. As an adopted child she'd never known the family she really belonged to, and in Sutton, Connecticut, she never found anything she belonged to either—the Sharanita Shop, the yoga, the Evelyn Wood Speed Reading had all come and gone. But whether she chose to take it over or not, she belonged here. That was what I felt she wanted not just Babe but all of us to hear. The asbestos shingles, the nasturtiums, the scorched lawn, it was less that they belonged to her than that she belonged to them, and she had Bebb's will to prove it. "To his surviving children is what it says," she said, "and I'm the only children he ever had as far as he ever let on anyway."

"I don't guess surviving was all that easy either, honey," Babe said, and the way he turned around to look at her beside him there, his plump neck contracted awkwardly by the closeness of the range, reminded me more of his brother than anything I'd seen him do yet.

"I'd never have made it without Bip," Sharon said. I remember her sitting beside Bebb that way in Armadillo once with the Holy Love cross blinking on and off over their heads, the setting sun turning their faces to gold.

Babe said, "He had a way with him, your old Bip, there's no two ways about it. It's why this place come to him instead of me in the first place. Why there wasn't a birthday Mother ever had he didn't remember her, and even when it wasn't her birthday he'd send things. There'd be picture postcards from the drummer hotels, and he'd ring her up, all that. For years it was me and Bert that looked after her hand and foot, but it was him that got the credit. Funny thing. You might think it would of been him that got the blame for not being there to look after her his ownself, but instead it was me that got the blame for not being him. His whole life long he fell on his feet that way."

Sharon said, "Except when he fell on his ass."

Babe clamped his jaws tight on that one. He raised both hands and let them drop to his knees. He said, "Bad news travels fast, and it travels far." He gave a fat man's sigh, like a tire going flat. He said, "I know he did time, and I know what he did it for. He had his shameful side to him the same as everybody else. The thing about your daddy was he could wink his eye at it better than the rest of us."

Sharon said, "He was always winking that eye of his," and it was at that point, without warning, that Babe did an imitation of it that made my scalp go cold because it was both so like and so unlike the real thing.

He let one eye flutter close, then open again, as though it had a life independent of the rest of him, but whereas with Bebb you felt that it was the rest of him that was in the driver's seat and the eye just momentarily getting into the act, with Babe it was the other way around. Just for an instant I had the feeling that it was only when I saw that one eye flicker that I'd caught a glimpse of whatever it was that was doing the driving inside Babe.

The last part of our conversation that rainy afternoon had to do with Jesus. Gertrude Conover was the one who explained how Bebb wanted us to do something nice for him down there, and Babe said, "Well, Leo was always big on Jesus," and Gertrude Conover said, "It was an enthusiasm I'm afraid I could never share."

She said, "Jesus was one of the great bodhisattvas, there's no argument about that, but I always felt he was a little bit of a snob. If you weren't a prostitute or a crook of some kind, he never had much time for you. He was the first person most people would have thought of turning to for comfort back in those days, but I never felt that way myself. The one I always thought I would like to turn to was Pontius Pilate. He was a very civilized man for his day, and he gave you a great sense of resourcefulness and strength, not unlike Nelson Rockefeller."

"Maybe so," Sharon said, "but it's still Jesus that Bip wants us to do something nice for," and we all thought about it in silence for a while.

Callaway, who had been standing against the wall as

narrow and dark as a grandfather's clock was the first to speak. He said, "Yucca mollentow cumble walla baptree," and I nodded thoughtfully right along with the others.

Gertrude Conover said, "Maybe so. Or perhaps there could be some kind of a playground for children. Or a vegetable garden. The vegetables could be given to the poor."

"Or you could set up a big screen and call it the Jesus drive-in," Sharon said, "Babe here could get some of his spacewatchers to watch if there's anything going on in the back seat."

"There's one thing while we're thinking," Gertrude Conover said. She had taken off one glove and was fanning herself with it. She said, "You never did explain how it was you knew to expect us, Babe."

What with the rain and the approach of dusk, it had gotten so hard to see that Babe went to the fringed lamp to turn it on. "I had a hearing on it," he said. He reached up under the fringe for the switch.

"A hearing?" Sharon said.

He turned on the lamp, and his face was lit up from beneath. "From outerspace," he said.

Gertrude Conover said, "You mean they actually come all the way down here to give you a special message like that?"

"They transmit them special," Babe said. Then, "Look."

Opening his mouth up as far as it would go and stretching it out sideways with his two forefingers, he leaned over the lamp so that it would light it up as much as possible. There was no doubt in my mind that it was the same mouth that we had seen the photograph of in the Uforium. As far back as you could see, each tooth had a black dot in the middle of it about the size of a mousedropping.

CHAPTER SEVEN

WHATEVER THE TRUTH is about visitors from other worlds, we all of us visit back and forth enough between worlds right down here, heaven knows. There is the public world, the world of things which happen more or less out in the open where people can see them. Babe's eventually explaining to us about his teeth, for instance; his insisting that we stay there at his house instead of putting up at a motel with Callaway; Brownie's somewhat disheveled arrival by air the next day, and so on—the sort of things that would get into your biography if anybody ever decided to write one. And then there is the private world, the world of things which happen inside your skin or which, if they happen out in the open where people can see them, are the kind of things that nobody would be apt to pay much attention to. Much of the time you hardly pay much attention to them yourself, and yet they are the things which make the difference between a good day and a bad day, things which in the long run may even have more to do with the difference between a good life and a bad life than the job you work at or the person you marry. I think of things like landscape and weather, things like the fact that there was only one bathroom at Babe's which we all five of us had to share, plus the sub-fact that the john seat wouldn't stay up on its own so you had to hold it in place when you were taking a leak, and how these things cast a faint but significant shadow over our whole stay. I think of the sound of Bertha's fly swat-ter. Like a newly grown moustache or the hum of a refrigerator, you got so used to it in time that you were hardly conscious of it, yet something inside you was always waiting like a fly itself for the next time it struck one of its deadly blows.

And I think of things more elusive still than those, though perhaps related to them. I think of a persistent feeling I had, for instance, that things both were what they seemed and yet were something else too, the way on the eve of our departure from Sutton I knew of course that Sharon and I were married, had had children, had come apart and together again; yet at the same time when Laura Fleischman and I were alone together for a moment, it was somehow she and I who were married all those years so that my unlived life with her and my lived life with Sharon challenged and menaced each other in unsettling ways. Babe was Bebb's twin brother, not

Bebb, and yet there were moments when, right in the very act of looking at him and cataloguing the differences between them in my mind, I would find that it was Bebb I was looking at. And Gertrude Conover. The more she tended to talk on about her earlier lives—often her accounts were much fuller than I have recorded them here, the parallels she drew between Pontius Pilate and Nelson Rockefeller, for example, going on at considerably greater length—the more I was inclined to believe that, as Sharon put it, the bulb was starting to go dim. Her stocking seams were not always straight any more, an occasional hairpin was left dangling from her blue curls. Yet who was saner than Gertrude Conover? Who better than she knew all the best short-cut diagonals to the heart of things: coming right out and asking if Babe had been to the moon, or coming toward you with that sideways tack of hers, looking at you half over one shoulder, which suggested always that she was taking the most direct route, the alternatives to which might involve two or three more lives to travel, two or three thousand more miles. Nightmarish is too strong a word but dreamlike maybe not quite strong enough to describe this feeling I kept having, and I sometimes think, looking back, that what triggered it was that moment before we left home when my nephew Tony for the first time held Lucy in his arms and in a single instant I knew that she was both my daughter and possibly not my daughter at all.

Brownie's arrival became another case in point. He got off the plane in Spartanburg looking just like himself if not more so—his Harry Truman sportshirt dark with sweat at the armpits, his sky-blue slacks, his white suede loafers—and almost before I saw him, I smelled him, the usual sweet strain of aftershave adapted for full orchestra, positively Tchaikovskian, as he came pushing through the glass doors with his smile hung out in the sun like laundry. Just Sharon and I were there to meet him—Gertrude Conover was making the most of our absence by taking a bath while the coast was clear—and Brownie embraced us both with if anything more than his usual warmth. He was full of his flight from Houston.

He said, "It was so peaceful there up above the clouds. I thought how when it's storming down here, up there the sun's always shining. It's like fairyland, and all the sad, cruel things that happen, they're like they never happened. If a man could stay up there long enough, it might give him back his faith again."

He listed slightly to one side at this, and I thought it was just the weight of his bag which he'd refused to let me take, but then I noticed how pale and clammy he looked and, despite the aftershave, the unshaved stubble on his face. When I tried to steady him, he pushed me gently away and setting down his bag took off his glasses and wiped around under his eyes with his monogrammed handkerchief. Brownie without his glasses is always an unsettling sight—like a nun out of her habit—and the more so because the heavy frames across their top keep a kind of lid on his smile which without them seems so helpless you're afraid a strong current of air might carry it away and Brownie with it.

He said, "I'll be all right in a minute, dear. I'm afraid I took a little something on the plane when the girl offered it. It's gone right to my head."

Sharon's voice rang with admiration. She said, "Why Brownie, you're smashed," and immediately I could see

95

she was right, but if on one level it made sense of things—the pallor, the starboard list, the aftershave so strong that he'd probably gargled with it—on another level, in the same near-nightmarish way, it threatened sense itself. Brownie smashed? Black white? Up down?

Sharon said, "Listen, Bip always said flying scared the piss out of him too. If a couple of belts help, why not?"

Brownie had sat down on his suitcase with his hairy bare arms folded in his lap and his glasses lying over one sky-blue knee. People had to walk around him like furniture. He said, "Oh I'm not scared of flying, dear. That's not the problem. When life doesn't mean much to you any more, death doesn't mean so much either."

It is not an easy thing to look miserable when all your teeth will do is smile, but it was one of Brownie's accomplishments. He said, "I had a talk with John Turtle before I left. I told him right out how the reason I haven't put on a service at Holy Love since Rose Trionka's wedding is because I'm not a believer any more. I can't preach faith of our fathers living still, dear, when my own faith's curled up inside me and died."

A porter wheeling a cart piled with luggage had to back and fill to get around him, but he didn't seem to notice. He said, "I take something every chance I get to help me forget."

So my private world as it existed down there in Poinsett for a while was a world marked by a kind of double vision not unrelated for all I know to the doubleness of having to use the john and hold the seat up simultaneously, a world in which I kept seeing a single, solid person like Brownie or Babe or Gertrude Conover pull apart somehow into two, the way if your stereopticon gets out of whack, the single 3-D view of the Grand Canyon, say, turns out to have been all along two views which only your gullible eye has given the illusion of unity. Brownie, that sugarcoater of all the bitterest pills of Scripture, his faith as ineffably sweet as his aftershave, went so queerly out of focus that beside him on his suitcase sat Brownie the godforsaken with his smile gone pale and clammy in the Carolina sun. It was with a great sense of relief that on the drive home from the airport, we moved back into the public world again, the world of getting from one place to another place, and I listened to Sharon describing to Brownie, who had the window wide open and the wind ballooning out his Harry Truman shirt, the solid, historical events of our arrival in Poinsett and our discovery of Babe. I don't know how much attention Brownie paid, but I paid plenty, held on tight to the reassurance that Sharon and I had both of us experienced more or less the same thing. It is when the public world begins to pull into two like the private one that the real nightmare starts. Irony is another word for it, I suppose—the good turning out to be the bad, the real the unreal. It is one thing to talk about it, but to run into it head-on is something else again.

Sharon was saying, "Like I mean you've got to hear this Babe to believe him. You don't know if he really believes it himself. How could he believe it?"

She said, "The UFOs, that's one thing. Lots of people believe in UFOs. They believe in them because they want to believe in them the same as they want to believe in ghosts or Scripture or real-life monsters. Bip was like that. He said to me one time, 'Honey, I'm a born believer. You tell me anything you want makes this world out to be crazier than it already is and one gets you ten I'll be believing it in less time than it takes you to tell it.' I'm the other way. I don't believe a quarter ounce over what I've got to. Life's a whole lot simpler like that, and it saves you being disappointed."

In the mirror I could see Brownie looking up at the bleached-out, hazy sky where he'd taken whatever it was he was only now paying for. He still hadn't put his glasses back on, and his face looked blown clear by the rush of hot air through the window. Beside him Sharon was so wrapped up in what she was saying that she didn't seem to care whether he was listening or not. Her hair had blown across her cheek and a strand of it into her mouth, but she didn't seem to care about that either.

She said, "Now Babe, he doesn't just believe they've landed. That's kid stuff. He believes there's millions more fixing to land any day. He believes they're going to come and take away everybody that signs up at the Uforium to a place where they wipe their tails with hundred dollar bills and there's shots you can get against death. He believes they've picked him out to be head of the whole show, and he's got this room full of moonrocks and burned up space suits to prove it."

Brownie let his head flop sideways on the seat-back, and taking advantage of his momentarily facing in her direction, Sharon pressed her point home. She said, "Brownie, that man's got him a special radio set right in his mouth. He showed it to us in his own front parlor. I thought I was going to have a hemorrhage. Would you believe teeth with transistors in them no bigger than that? Creatures from outer space installed them for him special. They wired old Babe up for stereo so they can ring him up any hour of day or night and tell him what's new on Mars. Jesus. I said, 'Babe, you've got to be putting us on,' so he opened up real wide and told us 'Listen.' "

We had all of us sat there in that parlor and listened. Callaway with his back to the wall, Gertrude Conover as if she was listening to the Budapest Quartet do Beethoven at the McCarter theater, Sharon like a lion tamer with her head almost in the man's mouth. The grandparents stared down bug-eyed from their oval frame over the sofa. The rain blew against the asbestos shingles. Somebody's stomach growled.

Sharon said, "Of course if you listen real hard, even nothing's got a sound to it. Only this wasn't just nothing. It was a kind of hum like a power plant. It was like what you hear inside a shell. Bopper, how do you think Babe made a sound like that come out of his mouth?"

I said, "I didn't hear it. I can believe it, but I didn't hear it where I was."

Sharon said, "Well, I heard it, but I can't believe it. I can't even believe Babe believes it."

I said, "Gertrude Conover heard it."

Sharon said, "Gertrude Conover's like Bip. She wants to believe stuff like that. It's how she gets her kicks."

Like a man coming out of ether, Brownie said, "What did the message in his mouth say?"

She said, "Not a damn thing. He said there was nothing coming through right then. Like the sound the TV makes before the Mickey Mouse starts."

I said, "What do you think about it, Brownie? UFOs. Martians. The whole scene?"

Brownie had put his glasses on by now, and they helped to pull him back into one piece again, the frown of the frames and the jubilation of the teeth coming together into the single 3-D Brownie I'd always known. He said, "Luke seventeen, dear. 'As it was in the days of Noah, so shall it be also in the days of the Son of Man.' It was the last sermon I preached at Holy Love. When the end is coming, you can expect many peculiar things to start to happen."

"You still believe the end is coming?" Sharon said.

Brownie said, "I would like to believe it. I would like to believe it will all end soon, and there are signs. There are many similarities between our time and Noah's time. I will mention only a few." To be talking about Scripture again after so long seemed to put a little of the color back into his cheeks.

He said, "For example, in Noah's time it says that men went away from the presence of God, and all you have to do is any Sunday of the year take a look at your ball parks and race tracks, your Disneylands and so forth to see that most people in this world just aren't very interested in God any more. Also it says it was in Noah's day that men started marrying two wives, and when you stop to think about what goes on in our own divorce courts these days, why two wives per man doesn't seem like anything to write home about. Noah's time was a time when Scripture tells us all flesh was corrupt, and I don't have to remind you what goes on in massage parlors, dear, or in porn palaces where they show things on the screen that give people ideas they would never have had on their own in a thousand years."

"Speak for yourself," Sharon said.

Brownie said, "There shall be signs in sun, and moon, and stars, dear. Maybe the UFOs and everything are one of the signs."

He waited until we'd arrived at his motel and Sharon was out of earshot to say what I suppose must have been on his mind the whole time. He said, "When you were there at Rose Trionka's wedding, you said something to me that's had me mulling it over in my mind ever since. You said Mrs. Conover told you she'd had a chat with Mr. Bebb—since he passed on, I mean—and you said as far as you knew, there was no way of telling whether it was just in her mind or whether—"

I remember him standing there in that cave of a motel room with the picture window at one end, the wall to wall carpet, the Hollywood beds, and hesitating when he reached that point. On the wall behind him was a big reproduction of a painting in colors that made your eyes ache. It showed a millpond with the mill reflected in it, weeping willows, blue sky, a boy sitting on the grassy bank fishing with his dog beside him. If I hadn't been somehow taught from the cradle to think that a picture like that was the last gasp, I might have thought it was the most beautiful thing I'd ever seen. I had a feeling Brownie might find it a comfort when he got around to looking at it later.

He said, "You said you thought maybe there was one chance in a million Mr. Bebb was still alive, and maybe if we came down here it could just be we'd find him. You said it might be he was hiding out down here from all the people who were after him those last days and

101

maybe he needed our help. It's why I came, dear. Just that one in a million chance."

With technicolor greens and day-glo yellows the artist had painted the woods stretching off into the distance on the far side of the pond, trees beyond trees fading away into a golden haze like a king's treasure, and I wondered what was so bad about an artist showing a world I would have traded this world for in two seconds flat.

Brownie was almost whispering now. He said, "I don't suppose you've seen anything that makes you think he's really here." At such close range the aftershave was no longer enough to camouflage whatever he'd had on the plane. He had reached out and taken my hand to steady himself. There were pinpoints of sweat on his upper lip.

I could have mentioned the man I'd spotted from the balcony in the Library of Congress and Callaway's nosebleed. I could have confided in him some of my more fanciful thoughts when Babe first came bouncing into the Uforium in his see-through raincoat, but any of that would have been to paint the kind of picture I'd been brought up to look down my nose at, so instead of a golden haze, I brushed in a cool, grey wash. I said, "I don't think so, Brownie. You'll have to see what you think yourself."

Out of the bathroom came Sharon's voice. She said, "Hey, Brownie. Guess what. They've got a blue light in here that sterilizes the seat in case of moongerms."

Brownie's smile glinted like spoiled fish in the shadows, and he released my hand. He said, "You can't be too careful these days."

He said, "If you don't mind, dear, I think I'll just lay down for a few minutes and rest my eyes."

That motel room of Brownie's became our secret meeting place, our haven, as the days went by. Callaway's next door was just like it and just as convenient, but it was Brownie's we always ended up in. Maybe it was the boy fishing in the millpond that did it. In any case the effect of our staying under Babe's roof was to make it virtually impossible to talk privately among ourselves about what we'd come for, and Babe didn't seem in any hurry to bring it up himself. He made little jokes about it instead. *See will Sharon let you turn on her dishwash, hear?* or *It don't do to rile up Sharon or you'll come home some night to find the door latched on you.* Little jokes about Jesus. *Where you reckon Jesus wants this sack of groceries put? Gertrude Conover, I've got a notion Jesus might be tickled pink if we dug us a swimming pool out back and asked the black folks over for a dip.*

The first morning we were there started with a joke about Jesus. It was still very early and I was dimly aware of chicken noises outside when I heard Babe softly calling my name in the hall. By the time I'd pulled on a pair of pants and made it out of the room without waking Sharon, he had gone downstairs. Peering over the bannister, I saw him standing there in what I took at first glance to be a spacesuit but turned out to be a sweatsuit that covered him from wrists to ankles with the hood tied under his chin and his big pink face swelling out of it like the sewed-on face of a doll. He was a man-sized kewpie doll beaming up the stairs at me with his hood going up in a point and his flimsy grey legs.

He said, "There was a fellow down here in a beard and sandals and a hatbrim made of sunshine asking after you. Said you were fixing to do something nice for him. Come take a little jog with me and could be he'll turn up again." So much for the joke, but in any event it was how it happened that the first time Babe and I had alone together was somewhere around 6 A.M. dogtrotting off across the scorched yard where the chickens skittered out of our way and then on abreast down the hard-packed, tomato soup-colored road.

I am a track man from way back and have coached it for years at Sutton High, but I was no match for Babe when it came to condition. Long past the point where I could handle any more than a few gasped syllables, he was still able to handle short sentences. He pointed out sights—shanty town, a pig farm where he and Bebb had worked as boys, a stretch of dusty hillside that he said was a favorite landing place for saucers. He talked about saucers, puffing, his eyes bulged out but the words still coming. He said, "There's some say I'm cuckoo. A phony. You name it. So what? Sticks and stones. It's the wave of the future. Hope of the world. Most folks I don't tell the half of it. Come see me in the office sometime and I'll show you things. Blow your mind."

He talked about Jesus. He said, "You thought I was funning you about Jesus. I was and wasn't both. Know something? Someday Jesus'll climb out of a saucer. Sunshine in his hair. Gather his own up just like it says. Only he's a spaceman, that's what. You'll see."

More for my sake than for his, I thought, he slowed down a little after a while. From a distance the sweet-and-sour smell of the pig farm was sweeter than Brownie's aftershave in the early morning air. We'd turned off the main road and were trotting through a pine wood, the needles so thick and soft you could hardly hear us. To make up for the reduction in speed, Babe was raising his knees higher, pumping his arms harder. He named names—*Red bud*—*Fat pine*—busting open with his ankle-high sneaker a mouldering stump all gold and henna and turpentine smell inside. *Stredwigs*—two or three squat, pitted gravestones inscribed Stredwig and set at crazy angles within the remains of a barbed wire fence, a couple of rusted-out cans. "Bert was a Stredwig," he said. "My poor old Shirley T. My sweet, hurt love."

He said "Thought the world of Leo. Close to killed her when he passed. The way she carried on. Snuck off to the mall after dark. Smashed Western Auto's window all to hell. They didn't press charges, thanks be. Some folks are all heart, and that's the truth."

He talked more about truth. He said, "Truth is it broke me up too when Leo passed. My own flesh I hadn't seen for years and now won't ever see. I had this dream. Leo was on a kid's swing. Funny thing. Says, 'No hard feelings, Babe.' Two times like that. 'No hard feelings, Babe.' He'd got this all-day sucker in his mouth so the words come out crooked and wet. He was the one named me Babe even though I drew breath five minutes sooner than him. 'Oh Babe,' he said. He tried to touch me only the swing pulled him out of reach. Farther and farther. 'Oh Babe,' he said."

He said, "The truth hurts. This will he left. When I heard he'd shot the place clean out from under me, it hurt. Not just the place. There's other places. But him being the one shot it. What if I didn't have a nickel to my name? What if I was sick and didn't have another place to go? I could have passed before him for all he knew and Bert left without a roof over her head. Her that always thought the world of him and him of her."

He said, "Well, a man's got to do what he thinks, and that's the truth. He left it to Sharon. Why not? She's his only surviving children like she said. Lucille Yancey never could have another one of her own. After what happened to that one she had." Babe stepped up the pace again. Through the trees you could see a black man in a white T-shirt hitchhiking to work, a woman dumping a pan of water out a window.

Babe said, "Death leaves a awful mess," jogging around what could have been a squirrel once or a cat or part of one of the Stredwigs. "Hell, so does life." The sweat had soaked through his sweatsuit leaving a Rohrschach-shaped stain between his shoulder blades. I wondered if the reference to the death of Lucille's baby was what had speeded him up again, his mouth clamped tight on it, his face grim: Lucille after a Tropicana or two too many had been wakened for the thousandth time that night by the colicky, merciless yammering, and had not even known what she was about when she grabbed up the first thing she saw in her rage and despair. Bebb had been off somewhere selling his Bibles, asleep or worse in some drummer's hotel.

Not slackening his speed, Babe said, "There's some might fight a will like that. Take for instance where's the papers? Was Sharon adopted legal? You got to have papers. There's ways to fight if a man wants to fight. Feel the old ticker ticking. Pumps the poison out. Who wants to fight? Kin fighting kin. Only a man can't help thinking. Sharon got proof she was adopted legal? Got papers?"

In sight of home again—we'd come a rough circle—he slowed down and wheeled on me, bouncing around me like a ball with his head cocked sideways and his guard up, jabbing at me with his right, that steaming tub of a man gotten up like a kewpie, a gnome. I made some kind of pathetic show of jabbing back. I could feel my pulse in my ears, my teeth. I said, "Don't worry."

I said, "Won't throw you out. Got our own place. Lousy shape. I've had it."

We'd stopped at the back stoop and I leaned over double to wolf enough breath to finish. I said, "Just needed the vacation. Plus what Bip said. The Jesus thing."

Babe had pushed off his hood and run his hand through his hair so that it stood out in rays like the sun on old maps. He said, "You hold on to Jesus, boy," and winked at me, blinked would be a better word for distinguishing it from what Bebb did. Bebb did it with one eye, not even knowing it; Babe did it with two eyes, knowing it well. The blink of Babe. Over the years I've seen it done by other people, other times. I've even done it myself. You catch the other person's attention—your son in the rear window of the car, for instance, and you on the front steps to see it drive off with him. Then you squeeze your eyes shut on the sight of him. It is more deliberate than a wink and takes longer, says more. It says *You and me, kid.* It closes everybody else out and

107

that one person in. So Babe to me anyway.

Eyes open again, he shrugged one shoulder high against his cheek to mop it. He caught my neck in the crook of it, and we were cheek to cheek there for a moment so brief it almost didn't happen. It happened. The rust-colored chickens clucking around our feet. The smell of coffee through the kitchen screen.

Sharon wasn't the only orphan. So what if he weighed two fifty, had farted on the moon, said rat for right? When he winked his wink and put his arm around my neck he was my father. I went begawking off like one of the chickens the second he let me go.

What I first thought I saw through the kitchen window was a balloon, a white balloon such as they print *Playland* on or *Happy Birthday*. What was printed on this one were the small, cramped features of Bertha Bebb. She was leaning over the counter getting break-fast. She hadn't put on her wig yet.

Sharon said, "I almost flipped when I busted in on her, but she didn't bat an eye." This was on our drive to meet Brownie's plane that afternoon. "She said it gets awful hot with it on summers. Just like that. She's not as freaked out as you think, Bopper. Soon as she spotted you and Babe tear-assing out of the woods, she said, 'You stand up for your rights, honey. Nobody loves you like yourself.' It's the God's own truth too," she said with her elbow sticking out the window and her hair full of wind.

Like Babe, she spoke of the truth as single, 3-D, not something that pulls apart into the two little Grand Canyons of the stereopticon slide, the right hand and left hand of the God's own truth.

I said, "Did Bip ever tell you anything about what went on when he adopted you? Did he ever happen to mention papers?"

"He didn't like to talk about it," Sharon said. "Like Babe said, Bip was a bag stuffed full of things he didn't talk about."

CHAPTER EIGHT

CALLAWAY HAD another nosebleed. He was driving Gertrude Conover someplace, and it started to happen so hard and fast that he had to pull over to the side of the road and stop. She said, "It's the worst I've ever seen him have. It was torrential. He has a trick of pushing up on that bone between the nostrils, but that wouldn't stop it. Nothing would. He needed his hand to hold the handkerchief so he couldn't drive, and I couldn't either, of course. I've kept my license up over the years, but I've lost that part of my nerve. Well, we were stuck there high and dry. What to do? Callaway said sometimes ice helped. Where to get ice? We were in the middle of nowhere. The only building in sight was a brick one with flat roofs and a smokestack like a crematorium. It was the local school. There were a couple of cars parked out front though school must have closed weeks ago, so I told Callaway to sit tight, and I would see what I could find. My dear, I found everything. A very helpful woman, ice beyond the dreams of avarice, a dishtowel to put the ice in. It worked like a charm. The nose was fine again. But now listen to this."

She said, "Do you know what those people were doing in that school? They were setting things up for a Well Baby Clinic, that's what they were doing. Of all the places Callaway's nose could have started to bleed, the one it chose was practically on the front steps of a place where in a very short time all the babies of Poinsett will be gathering." She paused to let this sink in.

Back of Babe's house there was a glider, the two benches facing each other with the little awning over them and the slatted floor you could push with your feet to make it swing. We weren't swinging, but that is where we were sitting, Gertrude Conover on one bench with Sharon and me facing her on the other. Babe was in the Uforium holding consultations. He said there would be people coming in and out most of the day, and it was true—maybe as many as a dozen or so during the course of the morning. It would be hard to generalize about them. A few were black. Some came with children in tow. By and large they looked like country people— leathery, faded, dressed for the occasion—but there were several I thought could have been Spartanburg gentry. There was a cadaverous man who was driven up in a pickup truck and had to be helped down out of the cab.

There was a black woman on crutches. I had been sitting there in the glider just watching the parade go by when Gertrude Conover started talking about the latest nosebleed, and it wasn't until her portentous pause that I started paying serious attention.

She said, "Of course you can never tell about the always-returners. When it comes time for the man in the street to be reborn, the matter is out of his hands. Everything depends simply on the shape of his karma. If it is a jagged, dangerous shape, say, he will be reborn as a Doberman Pinscher perhaps or a juvenile delinquent. If he has unsatisfied desires to work off, the shape of those desires will tell the tale. The timid little soul with dreams of glory will keep being born until he gets to be a Richard Nixon or the head of I.B.M., which is why so many of those high-powered people have timid little souls inside them and have to go to psychiatrists on the sly."

Without looking up from her reading, Sharon pushed her bare feet forward on the slatted floor and started the glider gliding. Gertrude Conover's chiffon scarf fluttered over her shoulder.

She said, "Well, the always-returner is a horse of a different color. He is so full of cosmic consciousness that he doesn't have any more shape than the air we breathe. What little karma he has left wouldn't cover the head of a pin. That means when it comes to rebirth, he is in the driver's seat. He arranges to be born wherever and whenever the fancy takes him. My dear, would you mind? It is making me feel a little giddy." She reached out one foot and placed it on the ground.

She said, "I do not believe in coincidence. I believe

Callaway's nosebleed is telling us that Leo Bebb has chosen to be born again in Poinsett, South Carolina, heaven only knows why. I believe there is every reason to expect that one of the babies that will be brought to that crematorium today will be him."

I said, "How will you know which baby?"

Sharon said, "There never was a baby born that didn't look a little like Bip till he got some hair on him anyway."

Gertrude Conover said, "Well, we will take Callaway with us. He is the canary in the coal mine. And we will take Brownie if he has recovered from his flight. I'm sure if Leo's there, he will find a way to make himself known to one of us."

Bert had appeared on the back porch and was scattering scraps of bread and lettuce to the chickens. "Heekie, heekie, heekie," she said in her tiny voice. With the sunshine on them, her arms looked as white as the bread. She had a pink ribbon to tie back her curls. "Hey," she said to Sharon, and Sharon said, "Hey, Bert." She looked as if she wasn't a hundred percent sure who Gertrude Conover and I were.

Brownie had recovered. We found him and Callaway having a beer in front of Brownie's TV at the motel, but they seemed glad enough to be interrupted. They had met only once before at the time of Bebb's funeral in the potato field, but it seemed to have been enough to establish a bond between them. Callaway had on an orange and lemon sport shirt so much like the kind Brownie favored that I wondered if he could have lent it to him. The way it set off his black face and spear-shape of bony black chest, I was able for the first time to imagine how he might have looked as a Pharaoh. Gertrude Conover didn't explain her purpose. She just said that we were going to have a look at some babies. As if making a libation to Ra, his face aglitter, Callaway raised his beer in the air and said, "Home fome bayseed tuffa," and then Brownie said, "Suffer little children." A translation? He made a stab at raising his beer too but faltered en route and drained it off instead. "For of such is the kingdom of heaven, dear," he said to nobody in particular, wiping the foam from his upper lip.

We spent a good part of that afternoon looking at babies—babies of all shapes and sizes, babies teetering in under their own steam, carried in, wheeled in. There were clean babies and dirty babies, tragic babies and comic babies. There were creamy, sleek babies and babies with violet circles under their eyes. There were little old men and women so clumsily disguised to look like babies that nobody was fooled. There were ladies with sharp yellow pencils and soft Southern voices to write down their health records, nurses and a doctor or two to test the hearing and urine, to examine the vision and blood of babies. There were classrooms set aside for each operation with the dwarf-size desks and chairs pushed off to the side where someday people like me would teach the wind out of their baby sails with maybe nothing worse than such somber verb forms as *if you had, might have been, will have gone,* let alone the grim metaphysics of irony, the helpless babbling in the presence of the unspeakable that is metaphor, the specter at the great feast of language that is spelling and grammar and the four major rules for the use of the comma.

Since Bebb's plane had crashed just about a year

earlier, any baby older than a year was automatically disqualified together with anybody much younger than a year too although, as Gertrude Conover explained, the one we were after might be less than a year because an always-returner didn't get hustled along from death to rebirth like the rest of us but could take his own sweet time about it if he wanted to. So we ended up looking at almost any baby that didn't show signs of five o'clock shadow with me hovering near the main entrance where they all came in and Sharon lingering between blood and vision and Gertrude Conover moving about pretty much at will, although she kept a weather eye on the parking lot as if suspecting that some baby might get only that far before losing its nerve. We all, of course, kept a constant check on Callaway's nose, and I made a special point of not losing track of Brownie either. I had a feeling that if anybody was to stumble on the reincarnation of Bebb it would be Brownie if only because it would comfort him so—a round, bald baby with a gimpy eye to look after and then finally, in his old age, to look after him.

I was struck by the way every baby has a whole collection of faces that he keeps trying on like party hats and how there's no way of knowing which is the face he'll eventually settle on for the long party of his life. There were one or two babies who looked vaguely like Bebb to me but there were times when they looked vaguely like a dozen other people too, so I made nothing of it. It wasn't long before, like wallpaper samples, they all started to look alike to me, and I stepped outside for a breath of fresh air.

There was a girl sitting on the parking-lot steps in skin-tight shorts and a halter with her hair up in rollers. She said, "You find the one you were looking for all right?" and then, when my only response was a blank stare, added the one word "Babe," which I heard as just plain babe, baby, the baby that in our madness we were looking for back inside that baby-filled school. She *knew*. So just for an instant the whole thing pulled apart again into two things. One thing was this local Daisy Mae splitting out of her pants and as much a part of the real world as the simmering black-top and the glare from the windshields of the parked cars. The other thing was the oracular utterance that had just come out of her moist little mouth like a comic strip balloon which seemed to confirm the reality of a world where messages from outer space were transmitted dentally and dead evangelists turned up in diapers to have their fingers pricked.

She said, "I heard you asking after him at the store," and the two things blessedly came back together again. She was the girl who'd been waiting on the old man when we'd asked directions and "had I found Babe" was all she meant. Even if she had given me back only an illusion of the oneness and solidity of things, it was an illusion I fell all over myself to grab hold of. Not having to explain the crazy business I first thought she'd been asking about, I leapt at the chance to explain everything else. Yes, we had found him. We were staying at his house. We were having the time of our lives. And "It's a shame about his wife," she said, only shame came out *shime*, wife *waff*, as she pulled a pack of Winstons out of her cleavage and lit up with a clink of her zippo.

She said, "They do say she's getting worse. That poor man. Most everybody feels real sorry for him. It's a

116

crime, the things that happen." *Crime* came out *cram* as she pouted out her lower lip to flip the smoke up toward her rollers.

I said, "Lots of people know Babe around Poinsett, do they?" except that I made it Points instead of Poinsett. Anything. Lots of people knew Babe. Lots of people had been to the Uforium. Lots of people had seen him toss his frisbies, had handled his moonrocks. I was like my hypochondriac ex-brother-in-law Charlie Blaine, who, if the electric lights happen to dim, makes sure lots of others have noticed it too so he'll know he isn't going blind or crazy.

She said, "There's other Stredwigs that were peculiar besides her. There was one of them used to set fire to people and lived under a bridge. Bertha doesn't set fire. She just creepycrawls around nights like a coon after trash. If she does anything real peculiar, folks don't make a fuss out of respect for Babe. Most everybody in Points knows Babe Bebb."

"And the Uforium," I said. "I suppose they know about that too."

She said, "They surely know about the Uforium." Leaning back on her elbows against the stair railing, she gave me a long look. She said, "They surely do know about that."

Then Sharon said, "She's got him spotted. You better come quick." Shoving the school door open with one arm, she almost dragged me in with the other. "Jesus," she said. "Over there by the water cooler."

He wasn't a well baby, he was a blind baby. His eyes were deep-set and flat like the eyes a child might push

117

into clay with his thumb. He looked about a year old to me, fat and pasty and dressed in skimpy shorts that his diapers hung down out of and a washed-out Donald Duck shirt that didn't quite cover his belly. He didn't look any more like Bebb to me than a dozen other babies I'd seen that day. He looked more like W.C. Fields if I'd had to say somebody. With one fist he was digging at his cheek as if it was something he wanted to get rid of, and his flat little eyes went all fluttery with the effort. Gertrude Conover was seated on a bench beside the water cooler, and the baby was on her lap. She had her arm around him, and I remember how tanned it looked against that rubbery little leg, how bright her gold bracelet. She said, "I know it's the one. The minute I saw him, the tears spouted out of my eyes," and Sharon said, "Honey, that poor little thing's enough to make tears spout out of anybody's eyes."

It's not just beauty, of course, that's in the eye of the beholder but friendship, love, everything that matters is there, and I suppose that's why in the twinkling of an eye they can vanish. What I mean is there was Gertrude Conover, that dear lady, to use the Wasp phrase, that one person in all of Poinsett who spoke my native language and came from the same Wasp world I came from and about whom my feeling was that if she was slipping, as Sharon said, it only went to accentuate the heights she still had such a long way to slip from—and then in a twinkling this all vanished and there instead was old, rich, dotty Gertrude Conover sitting by the water cooler as irrelevant as grape shears. As she looked down at that poor, starch-fed child in her lap whose diapers I could tell even at that range were in desperate need of chang-

118

ing, what she saw was a bodhisattva because that was a more manageable sight to see. It was myself, of course, that I lashed out at, my own similar distaste for reality as two-faced and double-crossing to the last drop: a baby, one, and blind as a bat, two.

I said, "When you're dead, you're dead. Christ. Bebb's dead. That's not Bebb that's crapped in his pants because the dead can't crap any more. People don't get to come back, and flying saucers haven't landed, and let's get the hell out of here." But of course all that was in the eye of the beholder too, and the next thing I knew it also had vanished and for an instant it was given to me to see Gertrude Conover more or less as maybe she actually was even when there weren't any eyes around to behold her—an eighty year old white woman with blue hair and crooked seams and a baby who looked a little like W.C. Fields asleep with his head against her throat so she had to hold her chin awkwardly high to accommodate him. There was a faintly strangled look about her.

She said, "What you say may be true, Antonio. We won't know till the curtain comes down on the last act. But in the meantime I'll tell you what I feel." She was talking very quietly so as not to wake the baby, and I had to bend down to hear her above all the clinic noises going on in the background. She said, "I'd rather be wrong about all those things you say and more or less alive and interested than right as rain and bored half to death."

It brought me to my knees or at least the baby did who without warning arched his back so violently that he would have fallen if I hadn't grabbed him. I took him under the arms and hoisted him up to where he was lying against my shoulder with my hand under his shirt to smooth his sticky, bare back. The smell of him was even more overpowering than his squawling. Gertrude Conover said, "You see. You're doing it too. Just like the time by the swimming pool."

Except that unlike the time by the swimming pool I knew that I was doing it. Even before she spoke I had felt myself doing it, the hot trickle down the side of my nose and around the nostril to where with a sad little burst it dissolved into the taste of salt. Only it was not because I believed it was Bebb that I was doing it; it was because I couldn't believe it was Bebb.

Gertrude Conover said, "There will be so much less to distract him being blind. Well, he'll find other ways to see, they always do. He will see things that are hidden from the rest of us like buried gold."

She said, "All the times I've seen him come and go, I've never held him in my arms before. It makes me feel very humble. Just think of it. The rest of us will all make a break for cosmic consciousness the first real chance we get, but not his kind. They keep coming back as long as there's a single straggler left down here to come back for, and you know how long that means, I suppose."

Brownie and Callaway had wandered up by then, and the five of us were all grouped around with the baby and me more or less in the middle so that you might have thought it was some kind of screwball baptism what with the water cooler right there and the way we were so quiet while everybody else was milling around dragging babies into classrooms to have their oil and water checked. You could have heard a pin drop if one had happened to drop from Gertrude Conover's blue hair as she rose from the bench, smoothing the wrinkles out of her lap. She touched the baby lightly on the sole of one foot with her finger. She said, "My dear, what it really comes down to is they keep coming back forever."

The mother turned up not long afterwards—a washed-out looking woman with big ears and a transistor radio around her wrist. Before she left with her baby, thanking us for minding it, Gertrude Conover got her name and address and the baby's name. The baby's name was Jimmy Bob Luby, and the last we saw of him was being dragged away backwards in one of those strollers that has a canvas seat you stick your legs through and a tray that comes down in front. He was sucking on the remains of a Milky Way, and like the broken clock that comes right twice a day, his fluttery little eyes looked just right with his expression of mingled apprehension and rapture.

We didn't get back to Babe's till dusk, having stopped on the way to drop Brownie and Callaway off at the motel where at Brownie's suggestion we paused to take a little something before supper. Once again we tried to figure out what if anything we could do or try to get Babe to do for Jesus before we started thinking about packing up and going home again. But nobody seemed to be able to keep to the subject very well—partly because of Jimmy Bob, I suppose, and partly, I think, out of a kind of unspoken sense that our simply having come to Poinsett was in itself such a major step on the way to doing something for somebody that we could afford just to coast along on it for a while. And the bourbon and gingerale slowed us down too, of course, that sickening combination of Brownie's which, as a strict Dewar's-on-the-rocks man myself, I would have ordinarily gagged at but which, its sweetness fading into the sweetness of Brownie's smile and Brownie's smell and the golden haze of trees in the millpond picture, lulled me sweetly.

Bebb was dead, I had said to Gertrude Conover in my moment of exasperation, and Jesus was dead, and though the exasperation was long since gone, the fact was with me still. The dead didn't care whether you did something nice for them or not, and there in that shadowy, wall-to-wall cave with my bourbon and ginger in my hand and vacation in my heart, I didn't much care that they didn't care. I had signed up with Babe for a consultation the next day—he had promised to blow my mind and I was interested in picking his—but I didn't much care about that at the moment either and found myself offering the consultation to Brownie instead. Having arrived only the afternoon before, he hadn't met Babe yet, and it seemed as good a way as any. He said, "That would be very nice, dear."

He was sitting on the foot of his bed with his glasses over his knee again only this time it didn't bother me especially—we were all of us nuns out of habit at that point I guess. "All those babies," he said, shaking his head slowly from side to side. "It's almost enough to restore a man's faith—like love-notes from Heaven."

Sharon said, "Down the old rat-hole, Brownie," touching his glass with hers, and no rat-hole ever came with so pearly and radiant a facade as the one Brownie raised his glass to.

So by the time we got back to Babe's there wasn't much daylight left and the peepers were peeping and when we pulled up in front, we just sat there in silence for a few minutes taking in the soft and twilight peace of it. The flamingos looked almost real on the front lawn and the asbestos house almost handsome with the pinewoods dark as a dream beyond it and the slope of hillside where maybe someday the celestial armada would land. I put my arm around Sharon's bare shoulder beside me in the front seat, and part of what my arm meant was that it was hers, this place, whether she ever chose to claim it or not, and I was hers too under the same conditions. It was a good moment, in other words, with Gertrude Conover dozing in the back seat, a faint whiff of woodsmoke drifting up from shantytown. All hell broke loose then.

There was a shrill barnyard squawk from the henhouse out back, a terrible thump and scuffling as the whole brood panicked, the coppery hens and cocks begawking out of there like the feathery end of the world. Then Bert—that bulky figure looming up behind the chickenwire, that massive grey head charging out of there with such force that the very air thudded out from her in rings.

By the time we'd pulled ourselves together, she was gone, and by the time we made it into the house, she was gone again if the house was where she'd charged to. Only Babe was there. He was in the kitchen, up against the refrigerator as if somebody had stacked him there like luggage. His face looked taken apart and put back together again by somebody who'd never seen a face. The mouth was on crooked, and the eyes were inside out.

He said, "She must have took a spade to it. It was the favorite one she had." By one yellow leg he was holding what could have been some ragged, rusted thing he'd mopped the cellar with.

CHAPTER NINE

IT WAS BABE, needless to say, that I went to sleep thinking about that night, but it was Bebb I woke up to somewhere around three o'clock in the morning with his daughter asleep at my side and the old house where he'd been born mumbling in the dark. It was a dream that woke me, a dream about Bebb.

He was sitting in a rowboat in the middle of the millpond in Brownie's picture. The light had the rich, golden quality of late afternoon, and the trees were glistening as though there had just been a rain. Bebb was in his shirtsleeves with the oars pulled back through the oarlocks so that the blades stuck up in the air on both sides, glistening and wet like the trees. There was a picnic spread out on the seat beside him. It was a white picnic laid out on a white napkin—peeled hardboiled eggs, sandwiches made of white bread, two glasses of milk. As though he'd been waiting for the right moment to do it, Bebb carefully picked up one of the glasses of milk and leaned forward to hand it to his companion sitting in the stern of the boat. His companion was Jimmy Bob Luby. The glass was all the child could hold, and he needed both hands to hold it. It was filled right up to the brim, and he had to lower his lips to it to take the first sip without spilling any. Bebb sat watching him with great interest. It was only then that I noticed the name of the boat printed across the stern. It was *The Venerable Bede*. I called across the water to him, "You mean the Venerable Bebb, don't you?" and it was the sound of my own laughter at what struck me as the richness of my joke that woke me. Bebb was laughing too. I suppose it was the creaking of the house that had worked its way into my dream or somebody flushing that one communal john.

The Venerable Bebb. It is appalling how few memories I retain from the catechism class of my Catholic boyhood and how still less I have tried to refresh those memories since, but a few hard facts remain. I have always remembered, for instance, that you are a venerable as soon as they start seriously considering you for promotion but that before you can make it all the way to the top there are three qualifications you have to meet consisting of a reputation for sanctity, the heroic quality of your virtues, and a few blue-chip miracles. It was these arcane matters and their possible application to the case of my late father-in-law that I whiled away the time with before I finally went back to sleep again. Thinking is an even queerer business than usual at that hour, of course —thoughts drifting off into sound or touch or flickering through your mind like somebody else's home movie, disjointed, sunstruck, leading nowhere—and my thoughts about Bebb kept turning into pictures of Bebb, hazy conversations with him in which the sound of his voice got confused with a crick in my neck or the sound of my pulse in my ear when I lay a certain way on the pillow. He sat there in his rowboat in the middle of the golden pond eating a sandwich so when he laughed at my joke, he almost choked, the white crumbs spraying out of his mouth like rice at a wedding and his eyes popping, then swallowing hard but with some sandwich still left unswallowed so that when he spoke it was like Callaway speaking—*vesper humdrum keyhole*—which made me smile into the crook of my arm at this second joke.

I thought, if you can call it thinking, of Bebb as venerable, a saint-in-the-making, and of the reputation for sanctity he enjoyed—would he have enjoyed it?—and what it rested on if it could be said to rest on anything. God knows there had been other saints before him who were queer as Dick's hatband, and a whole flock of them went cackling through the night like Bert's chickens— flagpole sitters, leper-lovers, middle-aged celibates in barbed wire underwear, virgins floating in the air like birthday balloons, grown men preaching to yellow-bellied sapsuckers or naked and cruciform in subzero cells. So why not Bebb with his penchant for baring

127

something maybe not all that unlike his soul, that holy lover of Trionkas, Redpaths, Badgers, Turtles, opener of suburban hearts, chief caterer and catalyst of the great Princeton feasts? If Bebb had run afoul of the law for his pains—the IRS, the Borough police, the fire insurance people—so had the others and fouler still, after all, for worse pains: sawed in half, grilled, tossed to the lions. I thought of Bebb and Mr. Golden a thousand feet up in their spit-and-glue flivver trailing *Here's to Jesus, Here's to You*, over the Nassau Street P-rade like restaurant ads, then the fiery martyrdom that ended them up corkscrewed into those starwise-scorched furrows.

The sanctity of Bebb was like a fish I was trying to hook, and I drew my legs up like a fishline so the knees touched Sharon, who moved in her sleep. I angled for the heroic qualities of Bebb's virtues that were moving drowsily, like carp, just below the surface. He hated heights, but I have a movie of him eating an ice cream cone on top of the Eiffel Tower as if it was his own back stoop. He was invariably sick in airplanes—he said, "Antonio, every time I fly, I puke, and every time I puke, I cry. Just like when I was a kid."—but puking and crying he flew all over the place anyway on the Lord's business and always took it off his income tax. Once at a tourist trap near Armadillo, Florida, called Lion Country, I saw him with my own eyes get out of the car and take a picture of two uncaged lions copulating not ten feet away, standing there bald as an egg with his pants caught between his buttocks and my camera pressed to his good eye because it was for me he was taking the picture. I remember when old Herman Redpath lay dry and brown as a smoked herring in his coffin, before the Joking Cousin took that leak on him which legend has it was his golden clew out of the abyss, Bebb spoke of him getting back on his feet again like Gene Tunney after the Long Count, and when I said to him, "Do you believe it, Bip?" he said, "Antonio, I believe everything," and when I said, "The way you say it, you make it sound almost easy," he said, "Antonio, it's hard as hell." So he was heroic in that department too, hoisting his faith off the ground grunt by grunt like an overweight weightlifter, the eyes bulging, the sweat rolling down. There was hardly anything worth believing that Bebb did not believe.

From far off in the night there was the sound of a shantytown radio or a breeze in the dark pines. Bert's chickens were mourning their tragic loss in silence, and miles away Connecticut floated in sleep like a raft with Lucy and Bill aboard, the puzzling, moonlit faces of my children. They were all right. Before we went to bed I called, and my nephew Tony said they were. He said also, "That Lucy, that Lucy" so I could all but see the marveling shake of his head, the Krazy Kat smile, as he spoke of my daughter or niece, his cousin or daughter, whom he couldn't resist naming to me twice that way— *that Lucy, that Lucy.* He said Charlie Blaine, his father, had dropped by on his way to a New York specialist. It was a ringing in his ears this time, or a sound like crickets or the hissing of damp logs, which he could get rid of only by shutting himself up in small windowless places. Tony said, "Christ almighty, Tono, he spent half the time he was here in the hall closet," and I said, "Good

God," thus exchanging long-distance blasphemies with my horny namesake who'd given me horns. Sharon murmured in the dark as though her young lover had wormed his way out of my dream into hers.

Bebb said, "Antonio, it's the enemies a man's got inside himself are a man's worst enemies."

He said, "There's dark and shameful things a man keeps hid that if he don't get them out into the sunshine they'll drag him into the dark." He stood there against the blinding stucco with his shame like a bunch of white grapes in his hand and pierced in a thousand places by the sun's arrows as the children skittered off barefoot through the seafood slops. He said, "It was a fool thing to do, a crazy chance, and I never blamed anybody it turned out like it did," landing him in a room not much bigger than the hall closet where he and Fats Golden spent five years imagining their way through black raspberry, burnt almond, pistachio, all Howard Johnson's flavors and then some. The Venerable Bebb. The crumbs flying out of his mouth. The glass of white milk he handed to Jimmy Bob Luby with such care.

I tried to remember his miracles then, counting them off like sheep. How he raised Brownie from the dead in Knoxville, Tennessee, unless Brownie wasn't as dead as he thought he was, and how he believed he might have raised poor Lucille too if the undertaker hadn't already done a job on her. How he restored the potency of Herman Redpath or such was the old Ojibway's boast and he claimed he could produce eyewitnesses. How he told the crippled son of Professor Virgil Roebuck of the Princeton History Department to rise and walk, and the boy managed a kind of fractured turkeytrot from his wheelchair to the center of the Alexander Hall stage where he fell into Bebb's arms like an armful of sticks.

Could Bebb have walked on water if he'd taken a mind to, climbed out of the rowboat and padded across the golden pond to me, turned the white crumbs into butterflies or restored the sight of Jimmy Bob? I said, "Old friend," skipping the words across to him like flat stones, "old father, old fart . . ." When they went zig-zagging slowly down to the bottom, I drafted a letter instead: "Dear Bip, Even if you never worked a miracle, you were a miracle, and that's what counts. I'll tell the *advocatus diaboli* to put that in his pipe and smoke it. I'll tell the *advocatus diaboli* we are going to do something nice for you in Poinsett, South Carolina. We are going to make a shrine to you where little girls in white dresses will sing the songs of Zion, and there will be piles of wheelchairs, wigs, dentures, white grapes," and I thought of Bert's poor chicken being carried into the shrine on a stretcher and of the way Babe had been stacked up against the refrigerator, then added to my letter *Diabolus, dillabolus, babilobus, babebulos*, pure Callaway again. Even I didn't know what I was talking about. I knew nothing else from then on either until I knew Sharon was leaning over me with her hair in my face saying, "Rise and shine, Bopper. It's time to get up." It was time to get up, the morning of what turned out to be one of our fuller days.

At breakfast Bert's face looked like a child's labored drawing of nose, mouth, eyes on a white page too big for them, and as the day before I had tried to read ahead from the faces of babies to their grown-up faces, so I tried there in the kitchen to read back from the overgrown face of Bert to what she'd been when she still had all her marbles and her hair, when she'd first known Bip. Then SMACK went the baby-blue swatter even as I sat there eyeing her over my Special K, and another redskin bit the dust. If you could have trimmed the page down to fit the drawing, I thought, it mightn't have been half bad— not pretty quite, but interesting, alive, clever even. Tipped there to the sunny window, it was white as the page it was drawn on, blue-lipped. She said, "Luby? Luby?" Gertrude Conover had asked about them. She said, "You know what her name is? Ruby Luby?"

It was the first time I'd seen her smile, as much a surprise as Sharon's smile. She said, "They're foodstamp people. And all those babies? No wonder there wasn't eyes enough to go round?" Like heekie, heekie, heekie, everything she said was tiptoe questions there were no more answers to than there were chickens in her coop that could answer them.

It was also the first day I really got a feeling for what it must have been like to live out a life in that house—the bare bulb hanging in the upstairs hall that had scared the wits out of the fat twins when somebody knocked it at night, the rusty claws of the bathtub's feet, the narrow back stairs steep as a ladder with old newspapers piled along the walls. Most of the wallpaper looked as if it went back to Bebb's childhood or beyond. In our room there was a diamond-shaped lattice with faded pink roses and brown dampstains that themselves blossomed into bigger, handsomer brown roses. Riding the same currents of air they'd ridden for years, cooking smells drifted along the same angled passageways and bald carpeting, through the same shadowy, varnished doors. Sharon showed me a room that Bert had shown her, tucked in behind the backstairs like a box with brown matchboard walls and ceiling as shiny as the doors and full of shelves. There were stacks of old magazines on the shelves, and brownpaper bags, blankets, linen, mason jars, hats and shoes and paint cans and suitcases, everything so neat and rich it could have been *trompe l'oeil* with the shadows like painted shadows, the spaces between things only the illusion of space. Sharon ran her finger across the front of one of the suitcases and in a startling imitation of Bert's tiptoe whisper said, "It's my treasure in there? She likes me, Bopper. She wants to show me her treasure."

I said, "Where her treasure is, there shall her heart be also."

"That's Scripture," she said.

Then after breakfast that morning I drove to the motel to pick up Brownie for his consultation with Babe, and it wasn't till he appeared dressed as if for a first communion in white shorts, white socks, a linen cap with perforated sides, that I realized what an occasion it was for him to meet Bebb's twin for the first time. He said, "Mr. Bebb never mentioned a brother to me. He never spoke about his family to me, and he never asked me about mine. We were not close in that way," and I said, "Tell me about your family, Brownie."

He said, "I never knew my father, and my poor mother had to put me in a foster home when I was eight. It was not a happy childhood, dear," and he looked so unhappy as he said it that I questioned him no further, just left him in the Uforium with two or three others waiting in undertaker chairs to see Babe.

Bert was hanging wash out on a line near the chicken coop as though it had nothing but the happiest associations for her, and almost as soon as I had introduced Callaway to her he started to help her with it. It was an odd thing for him to do without being asked to do it, and you could see the oddness of it sinking into her face like quicksand until it was gone. From that moment it was so much as if they were old friends that I sometimes think nothing less than Gertrude Conover's theory of reincarnation can adequately account for it—as if when Callaway was Pharaoh, Bert was a favorite concubine or a great white mare he rode if Pharaohs rode mares. There in the sunshine with their arms in the air they seemed to be hanging from that line like laundry themselves, he a long black stocking, she a sheet ballooning out in the summer air. Hidden behind the *New York Times*, my one line left open to reality, I could hear the sounds they exchanged if not the words, Egyptian words, for all I know, her anxious little question-marks, his dark syllables that stilled them like a hand.

A man came out of the Uforium carrying an open carton with what looked like a few of the moonrocks in it, and I wondered if Brownie's turn would be next. At some point Babe appeared in the window for a moment. He had pulled the yellowed shade to one side, and I could see his round face peering out as if he was counting the house before curtain time. If he saw me, he gave no sign of it, but I could see him see Bert and

Callaway. It was a long look he gave them like a time-lapse movie of an egg hatching—Bert first, Callaway second, then Bert and Callaway together, third. Then he blinked at them as he had blinked at me the morning we jogged: both eyes at once, deliberately, as if he was taking his movie and storing it away for some special showing at some special time. Then the shade fell back in place again, and it can't have been long afterwards that Brownie and he had their first meeting. Brownie told me about it at some length later that day, told me on a ferris wheel, the way things turned out. It wasn't an ordinary ferris wheel but a double-threat one with a wheel at each end of a single spoke so that not only did each wheel turn on its own axis but, as the spoke also went around, they were turning on its axis too, first one on top and then the other a dizzying height above the ground.

It was a county fair—part agricultural, part honky-tonk—and Babe had an exhibit at it, one booth in a great barn full of vegetables, farm machinery, handcrafts and 4-H demonstrations, where he had on display among other things the moonrocks that I'd seen carried out, the charred space suit, many UFO photographs and some round, flat things that Sharon called moonflops which were billed as plaster casts of outerspace footprints. Babe himself was on hand, like a life-size doll in his green jump suit, to answer questions and hand out flyers with his picture on them and a message entitled *There's Room for One More*, whose general drift was that when the saucers finally landed en masse for the great rescue operation, there would always be room for anybody who had gotten ready by participating in the Uforium SOS program—Shove Off Soon, Send On Spacemen, Save Our Skins.

We all went to the fair with him including Bert who I felt sure wouldn't have made it if it hadn't been for the fact that Callaway would be there too. She was dressed like a girl of sixteen in a skirt too short for her, saddle shoes and bobby socks, the usual ribbon in her hair. Babe said, "Keep an eye on her for me, old buddy," and I did for a while, on her and Callaway both side by side in the bingo tent among electric toasters, giant pandas, pink plastic cake-covers. But up there on that wheel I had eyes only for Brownie squeezed beside me on our swinging cradle as we revolved slowly through the stratosphere.

He said, "When I first laid eyes on Babe, I thought I was seeing a ghost. The blood drained right out of me and I must have looked like death because he took hold of my arm and helped me into a chair. He brought me a cup of cool water, and he said I wasn't to try to talk till I felt better. He said, 'Laverne, you look like you've been to hell and back.'"

Brownie said, "Nobody's called me Laverne for a hundred years, and how he knew I've been through hell, I'll never know. The tears started to come. I couldn't help myself when he called me by my right name instead of Brownie and showed me he knew what I've been through since I lost Leo Bebb and Jesus both in a single blow. He didn't hold my tears against me. He just turned away to the window so I wouldn't be embarrassed having him stand there watching me."

Up, up we went around the great, slow arc as though we were aboard a saucer already and bound for the stars.

The light was beginning to fade, and earth seemed far below us. Brownie said, "Babe told me many things this morning, dear. He told me about Jesus. He says Jesus was from outer space. He says he was a man just like us but from an advanced civilization. He says he came down to get us ready to go back with him to the world he came from, and when we wouldn't listen, he had to go back all by himself. Babe says the resurrection was really a spacelift. Jesus was the only passenger on a space-lift that was supposed to take the whole world."

I said, "Think of it, Brownie." What else could I say? For the first time in a long while Brownie's voice had something of the lullaby sweetness to it that it used to have when he was interpreting Scripture, and I didn't want to say anything to mess it up for him so I just said think of it and then tried to think of it myself. I thought of Jesus dressed up like Neil Armstrong for a moonwalk, rattling around in an empty saucer on that long trip home with all those empty seats that could have accommodated the rest of us. I thought of all the uneaten meals, the little paper bags with nobody to be sick in them. I pictured him sitting at the controls in his fishbowl helmet with his head tipped sideways like that da Vinci study for the Last Supper where he looks so tired and Jewish and some of the paint has chipped away.

Brownie said, "It's enough to make your head swim. Babe says Leo Bebb believed the same thing only he wouldn't let on he did because he thought people liked the old Gospel way better."

I said, "Do you think that's what Leo Bebb believed, Brownie?" I remembered Bebb in the basement of Bull's International Fireproof Storage, which was the last place

I ever saw him. Bebb told Sharon that the best words in all Scripture were the three last ones, and when Sharon said she didn't know what the last ones were, he said them out to her—"Come, Lord Jesus"—and I wondered now if what Bebb had had in mind was Jesus coming back in his saucer some day hardly gray around the temples yet thanks to those shots they had up there against old age and death and in the meantime communicating with this world through the fillings in Babe's teeth. And if that wasn't what Bebb had in mind, then I wondered what he had had in it. All the time I'd known Bebb, I'd never tried drawing him out much on what he believed. I'm not sure why, but I suspect maybe it was because though I was never much of a believer myself, I needed Bebb to be. I think I was afraid that if I asked too many questions, he'd turn out to have the same doubts I did plus a few more I'd never thought of because I didn't have that many beliefs to be doubtful about. I remember Sharon's asking him once if he had to bet his tail on whether the whole business about God was true or not, which way he'd bet it, and what he said was, "Honey, there's days I wouldn't even bet my green stamps." It was enough for me to get by on, the suggestion that there were other days too, but just enough, so I was grateful that the subject never came up in my hearing again.

Brownie's face had already started to recede into the dusk as though he himself was receding, so to reestablish contact I said, "What do you believe yourself, Brownie?" He heard me this time, and just as we reached the top of the arc and started down the far side, he turned to me and said, "Babe gave me a life-ray treatment this morning, and I believe it has already started to work."

138

If Sharon had been squeezed in between us when the life-ray was mentioned, she and I could have exchanged a glance and all would have been well, but up there in the air with nobody aboard but Brownie it seemed a tossup whether he was off his rocker or I was. So I just said, "Tell me about it," and he told me.

He said, "You have seen for yourself the things Babe has in the Uforium, but they are just a small part of all the things he has. He says he's got things that if they fall into the wrong hands it could put the whole world in danger. And he's got other things he says ordinary people wouldn't understand the use of any more than a cave-man would understand it if you showed him a copy of Scripture. He would just think it was something to start a fire with or throw at a dinosaur."

The sound of acid rock came floating up from the midway and a few lights had started to go on in the buildings where the agricultural exhibits were. The wheel stopped to let on passengers below, and we were stuck there about half way down the downward arc, dangling out over nothing.

Brownie said, "Has he showed you his life-ray yet, dear?"

I said, "There've been times I could have used a life-ray, but nobody's ever shown me one."

Brownie said, "It's not at all what you might expect. It's not like a death-ray gun out of Buck Rogers. It's more like a hairdryer. If you know what a collander looks like, it's like an upside-down collander covered with different colored wires coming up out of the holes like the inside of a TV. There are some dials on it, and there's an antenna on top. Babe adjusts it on your head and then

139

stands behind a special screen because he says you can get too much life just like you can get too much x-ray. He turns it on with his voice, dear."

I said, "What did he say to turn it on, Brownie?" and Brownie said, "All he said was just, 'Don't be scared, it's not going to hurt, Laverne.'"

I could tell that he was very moved, and for a few moments we sat there in silence while the wheel cranked down another spoke or two, then stopped again. He said, "It isn't a feeling you can put your finger on because it's more on the inside than it is on the outside, but let me put it this way. When I first started going to grade school, I was always very nervous the days I knew Mother was off working someplace. It seemed like I was lost and nobody was ever going to find me again the rest of my life. But there were other days I knew she was home because it wasn't her day to go out working, and those days I had a wonderful feeling I was safe and everything was going to be all right. Dear, the best way I can describe the life-ray is when Babe turned it on with his voice, it gave me that same feeling. For the first time in many years, I knew Mother was home."

I said, "Do you think the life-ray really did it or do you think it was just in your mind?" and Brownie said, "I know the life-ray did it, dear."

I said, "How can you know a thing like that, Brownie?" and Brownie said, "Because I've got proof."

He said, "You've probably never noticed it, but I wear dentures, dear." It was like Toulouse-Lautrec saying I'd probably never noticed it but he had this problem with tall girls. I had the feeling I was setting him up for some marvelous gag that I was the only one not to see coming.

I said, "I've always admired your smile, Brownie."

He said, "I don't expect to be wearing them much longer. Babe says very often the life-ray makes a person grow a brand-new set of teeth, and I think mine have already started to come in."

"What makes you think so?" I said.

He said, "I can feel them with my tongue, dear," and though I could not be sure in what light there was left, I have a suspicion that he did something then that caused his whole smile to drop an inch or two so he could get his tongue in under it and take a reading. At that point, having picked up a full complement of passengers I suppose, the wheel gave a lurch and was off in earnest not just on its own axis now but on the central axis too so that, revolving as before, we were caught up in a greater revolution still that carried us so high we stopped talking. Not even the sky seemed the limit any more.

For want of a nail the shoe was lost, for want of a shoe the horse was lost, then on to the rider, the battle, until in the end the kingdom was lost, as the old rhyme goes, because of that one lost nail. On such slender threads hang the destinies of us all. If it was true about Brownie's teeth, I thought, then it was true about the life-ray; if it was true about the life-ray, it was true about Babe, and what Babe said about Jesus was true, and it was true the resurrection was just a spacelift, then on until finally the Kingdom would be lost with a capital K. Thy-Kingdom-come itself would never come because there was no place and nobody for it to come from anymore except some other planet where a fart might carry you a hundred yards if you weren't careful. If Brownie was right about his teeth, I thought, then those days when Bebb

141

wouldn't even bet his green stamps on God would turn out to have been the only days he wasn't backing a loser. If Brownie was right about his teeth, then what was lost was in the long run all of us because saints and sinners, wise men and fools, we were all of us all dressed up with no place finally to go except death if we were lucky and a world where they had shots against death if we weren't. And of course if Gertrude Conover's theory of reincarnation turned out to be true, even if we made it to the grave, we still wouldn't be home free.

What a metaphysical ride it turned out to be up there in the Carolina sky with Brownie so full of new hope and me beside him with hopes dashed that I'd never even thought I had. The wheel became the great wheel of death and rebirth itself, the same vicious circle that had carried Gertrude Conover all the way from Pharaoh's Egypt to Nixon's USA, that had picked Bebb up out of the New Jersey potato field and deposited him in the womb of big-eared Ruby Luby to emerge with those flat little eyes I'd watched flutter as he gummed his second-hand Milky Way in the stroller. If Gertrude Conover was right that Bebb was an always returner, then never had he seemed more venerable to me. What sinister facts could the *advocatus diaboli* put in the balance against a man who postpones his own freedom in order to ride the great squirrel cage until he has rescued the last squirrel, which means postponing it forever? Around and around we wheeled with the bingo games, udder-pinchings, pie-tastings, moonrock-viewings, and skin shows going on beneath us, and when finally a man with a beer-belly and a five cent cigar raised the safety bar so we could get out, I could have knelt down and watered the red clay with my tears.

Sharon was there looking harried with a pink plastic cake-cover in her hand. She said, "Either of you know where Bert is?" and Brownie with the fate of mankind hanging on that porcelain smile said, "I could have kept going around up there forever," and I said, "The hell you could."

Sharon said, "Babe's having a hemorrhage. He says she oughtn't ever to be left alone."

"She was with Callaway the last time I saw her," I said, and Brownie pointed up at the wheel where about seven or eight spokes above our heads a child with a stick of cotton candy was leaning out over the side. Brownie said, "Watch out, dear. I think he's going to be sick," and he was right. I stepped out of the way just in time. It reminded me of the time the ice cream fell out of Bebb's cone on the Eiffel Tower and we watched it drip its way down from strut to strut as Bebb said, "Forget not the congregation of the poor forever."

CHAPTER TEN

PART OF WHAT gave our search urgency was that once
when Leo Bebb's wife disappeared in the same unexpected way, by the time we found her days later she was
laid out in a Houston funeral parlor with her mouth on
wrong and a dress that didn't fit her all that well either.
God only knew what had become of Bert. She could
have been anywhere—trapped in the Haunted House
among jets of air and spiders dangling, or flattened out
against the seat of the Arctic Bobsled as it gunned around
to the screams of the Grateful Dead, or being sampled
in the judge's tent like pastry.

Callaway was missing too, and Gertrude Conover,

Sharon, Brownie and I fanned out to look for them. Babe stayed with his moonrocks because that's where she would come back to if she came back, he said. His eyes were round as marbles and his smile was out of synchronization with the rest of him. He told us to try the ring toss, shooting gallery, cake raffle and so on because she loved prizes more than anything, but she wasn't at any of them or at the skin show either where two naked women were lying on their backs with their hands on their hips and their butts in the air tossing a beachball back and forth with their yellow-soled feet. We tried the chickens, such chickens as I'd never seen before, wild-eyed ones with Fiji headdresses, beige and tan herringbone ones, chickens with huge pantalettes and scarlet feet and lipstick-colored combs, but Bert wasn't among them, or at the hot dog stand, or resting her feet with her saddle shoes off outside the lady's room, so after a while we went back to Babe's, but she wasn't there either and neither was Babe. He had left Brownie to keep an eye on things for him and hand out the flyers. Brownie told us he'd driven home to see if she'd somehow made her way back there, and Sharon and I decided to go back and investigate for ourselves. Gertrude Conover was going to come with us, but Babe had taken his car and Callaway had apparently taken hers so we had to walk and told her we'd come back for her as soon as we could. We left her drinking a cup of coffee that Brownie had gotten for her somewhere, and I remember how game she looked perched there among the moonflops with her cashmere sweater over her shoulders and the paper cup in her hand. I suppose when you have survived the barbarities of Viking raids and died giving birth to a priest's child in a papyrus

145

swamp, an unexpected change of plans at a county fair is not apt to count for much.

It was dark by the time we reached the house, but there were lights on inside and Babe's car was there so we went in the back door and found Babe in the kitchen. He was sitting with his back to us and spoke without turning around. He said, "Your boy brought her home. She was here when I got here. I just got done putting her to bed." He was sitting at the kitchen table in his shirtsleeves with a cup of black coffee and a piece of chocolate cake with chocolate frosting. He stretched his hands out, one for each of us, and we each took one because it was impossible not to. He held us there for a moment, and I remember the black circle of his coffee against the white enamel table top and the larger black circle of the cake with his one piece missing. He said, "No hard feelings." When he spoke, you could see where the chocolate had blacked out some of his teeth. He said, "Like the man says, it's all well that ends well." He was still having trouble with his smile. It kept flaring up unexpectedly on him like a fire you'd thought was out. It wasn't till he said no hard feelings that I realized he'd held us responsible for Bert's disappearance, so I was afraid I was out of synchronization myself, and the conversation got off to a wobbly start.

He said, "She was all shook up. I could tell right off something had happened. She was sitting in here with five or six cigarettes smoking away in different parts of the house where she'd laid them down and forgotten. It was like they were parts of herself she'd left laying around all over the place so all that was left out here was an empty shell."

146

I said, "I guess the fair was too much for her," and Babe said, "It wasn't the fair." He cut us each a piece of dark cake and poured us coffee, sliding them across the table to us as though he was putting something together for us of which his words were one part and the things he was moving around with his hands another part.

He said, "Seeing her like this makes you think back. She wasn't ever Carole Lombard or anything in that league, but she had a sassy way of talking that beat all—nothing smart-ass but just all kinds of fun to her and a gleam in her eye bright enough to read by. There wasn't anybody in town that was better company than Bertha Stredwig back here forty years ago," and I wondered if he'd ever tried his life-ray on her and if it would start her hair coming back again the way Brownie said it had his teeth. He said, "There was a time she could have handled what happened here tonight like nothing at all. There wasn't anything or anybody she couldn't handle."

"What happened, Babe?" Sharon said.

He said, "Tell me about this boy of yours. What's he call himself?"

I said, "He calls himself Callaway."

He said, "What do you know about Callaway?"

I said, "He mows lawns and drives and has nosebleeds. Gertrude Conover says he has a lot of kids, and I think his wife left him."

Sharon said, "Tell him what he used to be in the old days, Bopper."

I said, "You tell him."

Sharon said, "Gertrude Conover says he used to be the Pharaoh. She says back in ancient Egypt he used to rule over cities that would have made places like Wash-

147

ington D.C. look like a whistle-stop."

He said, "Callaway brought her home because she said she wasn't feeling good. She shouldn't have ever gone in the first place. She was all wore out like I knew she'd be. Callaway followed her on into the house, and of course she didn't know what to do so she sat down someplace, her wanting just to go up and lay down on the bed. Then he plunked himself right down alongside her and set in comforting her. There's nobody can touch the colored folks for comforting people. They got it from their mammies. It's in their blood. The next thing he had a arm around her telling her never mind and she'd be better in no time. I'm not saying he meant any harm by it. I'm not one of those that say they're all of them no better than an animal."

As he talked, I tried to test the truth of how he said it was by picturing to myself how it might have been, and I found I could picture it well enough—the two of them propping each other up somewhere, those dense grey curls cradled against that bony black cheek, the rumble and creak of their voices.

Babe said, "Excuse me a minute." The phone was ringing and he went into the hall to answer it, which didn't put him far enough away for us to say anything but far enough away for Sharon to place both hands palm down on the table in front of her and look at me with her eyebrows raised as high as they would go. When he came back, he said, "That was spacewatch. They've spotted one up over Shaw Hill. Low, like it might be getting set to land. They're all excited it might be the big show."

I said, "Do you think it's the big show, Babe?"

He said, "Antonio, when the big show starts, it'll be like a golden rain. It'll be like the fourth of July of the world." He was looking up at the ceiling as though it had already started and in his face anyway you could almost believe that it had—that plump red face tilted upwards, those skyrocket eyes.

He said, "What happened was while he was doing his comforting, that hand of his started moving around places where it hadn't ought to move. She took to him the moment she set eyes on him, I saw that my ownself, but when he started cozying up to her that way and she could see signs he had more on his mind yet, it threw a scare into her. She tried to shove him off her, and there was a scuffle. She hollered out, and that time it was his turn to get scared. He was coming out of here on two wheels when I drove up, and my poor Shirley T., I found her in here with part of her shirt tore open and her wig knocked crooked, that pitiful grey wig she's got where once she had hair on her as long and pretty as Sharon's here."

He said, "There wasn't any harm done. I got her tucked in upstairs now. He'll be the hell and gone in no time and she won't ever have to lay eyes on him again. I'm not going to breathe a word, and don't you breathe a word either. There's no point making—" and then Gertrude Conover walked in looking a little haggard and chilly with her sweater buttoned up under her chin. "Another pot of coffee," he said, finishing his sentence, "Unless Gertrude Conover here wants some."

She didn't, poor soul, having already had coffee enough back among the moonflops where we'd forgotten all about her as Babe had unfolded his tale. Callaway

149

had brought her home, she said. It was a lovely, starry night and she had thoroughly enjoyed herself though she was glad she'd brought along her sweater. She and Brownie had handed out a lot of the Uforium flyers, and when Callaway showed up to get her, he had helped them for a while. Sharon asked her about Callaway then—in a guarded way, as the expression goes, and I remember thinking how there was hardly one of us she wasn't somehow guarding.

She said, "Callaway mention how he was the one that took Bert home?" and Gertrude Conover said, "She got a little overtired and weepy, poor dear, and it was Callaway she turned to. He was very proud. You'd have thought she'd given him the shirt off her back. What a world it is."

Sharon was formulating a new and even more ponderously guarded question when Babe intervened. Gertrude Conover was standing behind his chair so she couldn't see him give a microscopic shake of his head to silence Sharon as effectively as if he'd clapped his hand over her mouth while Gertrude Conover continued with what a world it was.

She said, "Well, I saw Ruby Luby again, that name. She must have had six children with her, all obviously hers with those big ears and all under six years old, I would swear. It was far, far past their bedtime, of course, and you've never seen such a miserable little contingent dragging along behind her, their faces all smeared up with soda pop and ghastly candy bars. Except Jimmy Bob," and over Babe's red head she faintly narrowed her eyes at us so that this time it was about Jimmy Bob that we were silenced, a whole new set of secrets guarded.

150

She said, "He was as grimy as the rest of them, but he was radiant. He was enthroned in his little stroller like the Dalai Lama with all the sacred marks upon him and his face positively giving off light like the moon. He is blind as a bat, poor thing, but you can tell by just looking at him that he sees things the rest of us don't even dream. I bowed my head to him as his mother wheeled him by, and I know in some way he saw me. He turned his little head toward me and nodded back so gravely it was as if he was saying, 'There you are, Gertrude Conover.' My dear, it was as if I could actually hear him say, 'There you have always been, Gertrude Conover, and there you are again.'

"Well," she said, "I am getting a little overtired and weepy myself, and this is as good a time as any to have my go at the bathroom before the line starts forming."

Later that night, in bed among the brown roses, I decided that what Babe had been doing with all the words he had spoken and the things he'd moved around the table was less putting something together than burying something for us to find when the time came, less telling us about something that had happened than telling us about something he wanted to happen so bad he could taste it like the chocolate on his teeth. It was why he couldn't keep a lid on his smile. I woke Sharon up to explain it to her. I said, "He wants us all the hell out of here, that's what he's saying. He's saying it doesn't matter about any will. It's his place and we've hung around long enough. He's using Callaway to get rid of us, and it doesn't matter whether Callaway really went ape or not.

I say we get the hell out before we get caught in the fourth of July of the world."

Sharon said, "I say it's my place, and I'll get the hell out when I'm ready to get the hell out."

"What's the point?" I said, and Sharon said, "There doesn't have to be any point. Bip left me this place, and maybe there's something here I can use. Maybe we'll even find something nice to do for Jesus after all."

I said, "Maybe the nicest thing we can do for Jesus is get Callaway out before they string him up."

She said, "We don't string them up so much anymore, Bopper."

I said, "Do you think he really did it?"

"With Bert?" she said. "Listen, that Babe's got it in his head everybody's some kind of kook. He said plenty about Bip too after you went up."

"Such as," I said.

"He said Bip didn't get his kicks like other people," she said, "and when I asked him what else is new, he said he didn't just mean he was a flasher, like what they sent him up five years of his life for. He didn't come right out and say so, but he let on there were some that thought he and Brownie had a thing going way back. He said the reason Luce started hitting the Tropicanas was because she knew about it. Jesus."

I said, "Do you believe it?"

As she moved her head toward the window, her cheek turned silver, and she placed the back of one hand against it. She said, "There was lots about Bip I didn't ever know or see. Like I never saw him bare but once in all my life. Once when Luce was smashed she said she never saw him bare except a few times in all her life either. It was winter the time I saw him. I went into his room to look for something, and he was laying there naked as the day he was born. I thought he was dead, and I don't know to this day what he was up to. It was cold in that room, and he was staring straight up at the ceiling with those jellybean eyes of his. He had dimply knees and not a hair on him except a little where you'd think and not much else there either that showed anyway with the pot he had on him. It was so cold in there I guess he'd all just shriveled up. He had his arms down stiff at his sides and his legs out straight like he was made of snow. I was still a kid, and I went running downstairs and said, 'Oh Jesus, Luce, they got my daddy laid out dead on his bed,' and Luce said, 'That's what you think.' Half the time I don't think she knew what he was up to any more than I did. There wasn't anybody knew all there was to know about Bip."

"Including Babe," I said.

She said, "If there's things to know about Bip that Babe knows, I want to know them. It's like maybe that's the main thing he sent us down here for."

I said, "Maybe Babe was the one thing he didn't have the guts to flash till after he was gone."

"That Bip," she said. "Nobody could ever tell what he was fixing to do next."

"Babe too," I said. "Poor Callaway."

"Poor Bert. Poor everybody," Sharon said. "Poor Bip in that stroller saying, 'There you are again, Gertrude Conover.'"

"Forget not the congregation of the poor forever," I said, and lifted a ribbon of silver hair from the glistening silver cheek where her hand lay.

153

CHAPTER ELEVEN

BROWNIE SAID, "I've got good news and bad news, dear,"
and I said, "Better hit us with the good news first,
Brownie," and then Brownie did for sure the same thing
with his smile that I'd suspected him of doing on the
ferris wheel the day before. The whole smile dropped
about an inch, and suddenly it was not Brownie any
more but Lon Chaney changing from Dr. Jekyll to Mr.
Hyde with this terrible maw of fangs hanging out over
his lower lip. My double vision again, one pulling apart
into two.

Fortunately the others couldn't see him from where
they were sitting in that dark cave of a room where the

only bright and cheerful thing was the golden millpond above Brownie's bed. It seemed a crime to be inside on the loveliest day we'd had yet—clearer and cooler for a little rain the night before, the red roads a deeper and less dusty red, the greens greener—and of course it was the question of Callaway's crime that had brought us together there to conspire like criminals at a safe distance from the innocent Babe, who, even as we'd slid out of the drive on muffled wheels, had been putting on one of his shows. The Uforium blinds were all drawn, and you could hear the extraterrestrial blips and chirpings, the canned voice starting out on its spiel as the lights spun.

Brownie said, "They have definitely started to come in. I can feel them with my tongue. The life-ray is working, dear. It won't be long until I have to stop wearing my dentures because they won't fit down over the gums anymore." All of this came out thick and clattery like an eggbeater, but then he snapped the smile back in place again. He said, "It may not mean much to you, but it is very good news to me," and I said, "It means more to me than you know," because what it meant, of course, was that if the life-ray worked, then Babe worked, and if Babe worked, then Jesus was Neil Armstrong and Thy Kingdom Come was a five hundred yard fart and an anti-death shot in the ass on the Planet of the Apes.

Sharon said, "You better lay the bad news on us too, Brownie," and Brownie said, "Maybe I better let Harold tell you about that himself." I don't think even Gertrude Conover could think for a moment who Harold was until he started talking. Harold was Callaway. Harold Callaway. It was like being at a christening.

Callaway said, "Buffa. Waffle. Tomtom. Kudzu. Clapper," short, heavy syllables that came thumping out like footsteps as Callaway sat there on the foot of one of the twin beds staring down at the wall to wall carpet with his head in his hands. I have never seen a shirt as gorgeous as the one he was wearing—a fireman's red covered with psychedelic green cabbages or brains that Tutankhamen himself would have been pleased by let alone Harry Truman. Out of his breast pocket he pulled a piece of paper which he unfolded and handed to me.

The paper showed a crudely drawn picture of a naked black man. Around his neck hung something that looked at first glance like that ancient Egyptian symbol of life and happy days the *ankh* but that proved to be the parts of himself that should have been located at his crotch. What was located at his crotch instead was a kind of madman's tu-tu of dark, heavy lines scrawled around and around as if to obliterate some unforgivable mistake. In one place the pencil had gone through the paper. Underneath was written in block letters NIGGER GO HOME, and Brownie said, "He found it slipped under his door when we got back from breakfast." Then Callaway said something, and Gertrude Conover said, "Maybe somebody booked it in advance," and Callaway shook his head. Brownie said, "I said he could move in with me if his was spoken for, but the man said he couldn't allow it because this isn't a double room. I told him it has twin beds in it, but he says that doesn't matter. He says when a room's got just one person in it, that makes it a single room and he can't put two people in a single room. We got talking in circles, dear. It's as plain as the nose on your face they're throwing him out."

156

I don't remember ever having seen Callaway smoke before, but he had lit up by then and was sitting there with a king-size cigarette expertly angled up from his lips to keep the smoke at a distance. In contrast to the dead white of the cigarette, the whites of his eyes looked like meerschaum. It was Sharon who asked him the unaskable then and asked it in front of Gertrude Conover and Brownie, neither of whom had heard a word of Babe's charges either, so that she was confronting all three of them at the same time. She said, "When you took Bert home last night, Callaway, did anything happen between you and her that might have made things turn out like they have because Babe said when he got home she was all shook up with lighted cigarettes smoking all over the house where she'd left them." It was a long, unraveled sort of sentence that ended up somewhere between a question and a statement, and it came through as both a grave question that demanded a grave answer and also as a promise that no matter how he answered, there would be time to talk about it afterwards. It was as hard a thing as I suppose she had had to do up to that point, and I remember thinking that as recently as a week before I couldn't have imagined her doing it and that maybe the reason she was able to do it then was that for the first time in her life she had a base to do it from. She was asking about something that had happened in a house that was her house because Bebb had left it to her, so the house was her base, and in some queer way I suspect that Babe and Bert may have been her base too. They were hardly a pair to give you a sense of security, but they were more in the way of a family than she'd ever known she had before, and I think that counted for a lot with

157

her. She sat on the edge of Brownie's dresser among the deodorants and aftershaves while he and Gertrude Conover and I waited in various kinds of silence for Callaway to answer.

He had risen from the bed and stood in profile at the picture window with his hand on his hip and the scurrilous drawing in his hand so that it projected forward not unlike the way the kilts of pharaohs are depicted on sunbaked walls as projecting forward, which I have read somewhere is supposed to indicate that those ancient fathers of their people were so potent as to be in a perpetual state of erection. He stood there all black and bony and fireman's red against the parking-lot view and for a few moments said nothing at all. Then he said something short and deep and the texture of plaited straw at the end of which he raised the drawing in both hands and with ritual precision tore it in two and then each of the pieces in two and then dropped it in the basket by the door.

Such was the potency of the gesture that even without the faintest idea what he had said, I could not doubt his innocence of Babe's charge, and it was obvious that none of the others doubted it either. Gertrude Conover said, "The reason I have always called you Callaway was not to demean you but because, as you know, my husband's name was also Harold, and when he was still alive it was confusing to have two Harolds around at the same time. The alternative was to call my husband Conover."

Following on what had just passed, Callaway's handsome smile came as a special gift. "Thalassa jubal," he said, and this time it was Gertrude Conover who smiled.

"It's quite true," she said. "Sometimes I did call him Conover."

In other words unless either for reasons of her own or out of the depths of her confusion and unreason Bert had lied to Babe about Callaway, then Babe must have lied to us about him. And now both the drawing under the door and the threat of eviction seemed to prove that he was spreading the lie around. Why? To get us all the hell out. Why? Because we'd been there long enough. Because Sharon had a claim on his house which he didn't know what to do about. Because he'd had a hearing on it from outer space. Maybe just because he was Babe and as inscrutable in his way as Bebb had been inscrutable in his. I thought of Babe's see-through raincoat through which you could see nothing but the next garment down and how there was probably nobody anywhere who wasn't both what you could see he was and also what you could not see he was, like buried treasure or buried trash. So there in that dreary motel I had the sense all over again of everything pulling apart until the world itself pulled apart into the world where words are spoken and deeds done and the other world where words are left unspoken and deeds only dreamed or done in secret and matters as small as having to hold the seat up and take a leak at the same time can cast over a man's life a pall or a radiance too vast to measure.

And I thought of the faith Brownie had lost and the new faith in Babe he had found to take its place and how to launch a counterattack against Babe for having borne false witness would be to risk demolishing the only radiant thing Brownie had left, inside or outside, except his smile. So I didn't launch anything and neither did the others, still vibrating as they were from Callaway's eloquence. Instead, like the man at the complaint desk, I said only that there must have been some mistake and it probably wasn't anybody's fault, and Sharon said the hell it wasn't, and Gertrude Conover said if this motel forced Callaway out, she was sure there must be other motels that would take him in, and Brownie said "I think the root of the trouble is Bertha Bebb herself. For years she has gone around breaking things. Now she is taking a turn at breaking people. It isn't her fault, it is just the way the poor soul is. I'm sure Babe will be able to straighten everything out." Maybe it was because I suddenly found myself hoping against hope that he was right on both counts that I said I would go see him immediately myself and have the consultation I had already put in for. At the same time, though I wouldn't have threatened Brownie's faith for anything, I couldn't resist at least holding it up to his own inspection. I said, "I wonder why he hasn't ever given Bert a go-round with his life-ray," and Brownie said, "Oh, but he has. He told me about it."

"What did it do for her?" I said, and Brownie said, "It made her hair fall out, dear."

Babe said, "It's the Plymouth Rock of the future. It's the first place they'll set their foot down. It's the spot where the new world's going to start at." It was Shaw Hill, the slope where spacewatch had logged its sighting the night before. Babe looked like an attendant from a Turkish bath, pale and squinty in the bright sun. He was wearing a T-shirt, a voluminous pair of khaki shorts, and sneakers without socks. He was leaning against the post of a broken-down barbed wire fence and I was leaning on my elbow in the grass. I had told him about the drawing and what it showed hanging around Callaway's neck like an ankh and about the circular conversation Brownie had had on the subject of what constituted a double room and about how Callaway had protested his innocence. It placed the ball as squarely in his court as a ball can be placed, I thought, but instead of lobbing it back at me, he merely pocketed it with that slow, two-eyed blink of his as if he was putting it away to be dealt with later, or putting me away. Then he said his piece about Shaw Hill's being the Plymouth Rock of the future and left me to conjure up visions of whatever creature would be the first to set spacefoot on it or webfoot, claw, golden sandal, to inaugurate the new age. Then he opened his mouth wide enough to reveal the mousedroppings and said, "Don't fret over Callaway. All things work together for good to them that love God, Antonio," and immediately two things worked together for me with a force I can't overestimate. One thing was that his lips didn't seem to move while he was speaking, and the other thing was that the voice he spoke in was Bebb's voice. For the moment I could think of only one explanation, and that was that Babe was Bebb.

I didn't see how it was possible, but every alternative seemed impossible. Babe had been Bebb right along. He was Bebb now. He was quoting Scripture. He was playing a game I didn't understand, but that was the kind of game Bebb had always played. The only thing that couldn't be Bebb was the hair because Bebb was bald as an egg. The hair couldn't be real. As surely as I knew he was Bebb, I knew that that rusty red hair must be, like Bert's, a wig.

To throw the custard pie, to burst in naked on the beautiful stranger, to laugh at funerals—one way a man defines himself is by the impulses he doesn't act on, and I was born into a world where that was so much the preferred way that its alternative was almost literally unthinkable. Yet here for once it was the alternative I chose. I had the impulse, and I acted on it. Before either of us knew what was happening, I reached out and took hold of a spike of Babe's red hair and gave it enough of a tug to pull the wig off and expose that bare and shiny scalp I knew so well. It was an act of madness, and even as I was doing it, I knew it was, knew that I had finally fallen apart into two myself: both a madman and a man watching himself be mad. Time stopped in its tracks, and the moment fell clear like a frame from a comic strip— the round, pale man leaning against the post, and me with a spike of his hair in my hand and a comic strip balloon over my head full of exclamation points and question marks.

The hair didn't come off, and the voice that spoke wasn't Bebb's. It was Babe's. It said, "Got my own teeth too." I said, "Who are you anyway for Christsake?"

I said, "Do you expect me to believe you've been to the moon and had little green men put transistors in your teeth? Do you even expect me to believe you believe it? Do you think I'm crazy? Are you crazy yourself?"

He said, "They're not green, and I'm no crazier than the next man, and as for you, Antonio, I don't know what I think exactly about you. I'm just a country boy.

The moon? Listen," he said. "I'll tell you something. The moon's nothing next to the places I've been. Hell, they're not even places like the moon's a place or this hill's a place. Is a dream a place? Is there a place inside you where you live and watch the world out of through your two eyes? Are the things a man remembers out of his life a place he goes to like you go to the pictures Saturday night? I've been where there's no maps to show the places they're at because they're no more places than tomorrow's a place. I tell about the moon because there isn't a mother's son would believe it if I told the truth about the other places I've been and the things I've seen there don't have a shape or edges to them like a stick of wood."

Opening his mouth, he stuck two fingers in it to spread the lips apart and pulled it sideways. Like a man talking to a dentist, he said, "Do you think I just went down to old Doc Hansel on Henrietta street and said, 'Fix me a black filling in each one of these here so I can bluff a bunch of dumb rednecks?' Listen," he said, taking his fingers out, and once again, without any apparent movement of his lips, Bebb's voice came out.

It said, "Everything's going to end up making sense. You'll see. There's a time coming when the wolf and the lamb will feed together, and the lion shall eat straw like the bullock, and dust shall be the serpent's meat."

It said, "Antonio, there'll come a day they shall not hurt nor destroy in all my holy mountain, saith the Lord."

I said, "What are you, some kind of outerspace ventriloquist?"

I said, "I ask you about Callaway, and you pull one of

163

your crazy stunts. That man's innocent as the day, and you're spreading it around he tried to jump your wife."

Babe said, "That's what your old Bip's telling you. He's saying it's all going to come out in the wash who's innocent and who's guilty. Who is which and which is what, you'll find it all out when the time comes. Meantime, stay loose. Do like Bip says, and the time will come."

I said, "You want us to get the hell out of here, and you're lying in your teeth about Callaway to help us on our way."

He said, "Listen," and again there was the sound of Bebb's voice. Bebb's voice? There wasn't that much difference between the two voices really—Bebb's a little quicker, crisper than Babe's with not quite so much Poinsett in it, but nothing a twin brother couldn't handle if he half tried. As for the lips not moving, I've seen any number of amateur Edgar Bergens do as well. Yet it was as if the voice was coming through Babe's mouth instead of out of it, and it wasn't just the way it sounded that was like him but the things it said. There had been times when I had known Bebb to keep up his end of a conversation with almost nothing but scriptural quotations, and that was what he seemed to be doing again.

He said, "And God shall wipe away all tears from their eyes, and there shall be no more death, neither sorrow nor crying, neither shall there be any more pain, Antonio, for the former things are passed away," and for a moment I found myself reacting to it as if it was not just a clever impersonation but a real message from Bebb if not Bebb himself, and I said, "Jesus, Bip, don't think I wouldn't believe it if I could," and he said, "Antonio, you'll believe it when He comes," and I said, "Oh shit, Bip"—*shit* not as an expletive but as a cry of longing and despair that welled up not just out of Callaway's getting screwed but out of the whole world's getting screwed, out of all sadness, failure, loss. "Poor everybody" Sharon had said among the brown roses, and Brownie, Jimmy Bob, my nephew Tony with the baby in his arms, everybody was included in my excremental lament. I said, "He's been coming two thousand years, Bip, and he hasn't made it yet."

"He'll make it," Bebb said. Then Babe said, "Hi-yo Silver," and then "Brrrrum brrrrum brrrrum bum bum" in strenuous imitation of the overture to *William Tell* by Gioachino Rossini.

I suppose what happened next can be put down to a number of causes of which the life-ray, however it's to be finally understood, has got to be one. Babe hadn't brought the upside down collander with him that Brownie had described to me on the ferris wheel, but he said he didn't need it. He said they'd built the life-ray power into him the same way they'd built the transistors into him, and all he had to do was activate it. Then right there on Shaw Hill, that Plymouth Rock of the future where they shall not hurt nor destroy in all my holy mountain saith the Lord, he activated it. He fixed me with those gumdrop eyes of his and reached both his hands out toward me with the fingers arched over as if he was taking hold of a pair of doorknobs, and activated it with the same words he'd used on Brownie. "Don't be scared," he said, and I wasn't.

In the candlelight voice of Liberace at the keyboard, Brownie had said it made him feel Mother was home, and it made me feel as if I was home myself. I felt the way I used to feel when my sister Miriam and I were children in New York in wintertime, and it was dusk, and many stories below on Park Avenue the traffic was honking its way slowly home from work like cows at milking time while up in our bedroom we had the radio on to Omar the Mystic, Uncle Ezra, Easy Aces, the Lone Ranger. And there was the smell of supper in the air, and there was nothing bad or sad anywhere in the world that could ever get at us. That was how the life-ray made me feel when Babe activated it by saying, "Don't be scared" and turning two invisible doorknobs in the air.

It was Babe who'd planted the Lone Ranger in my mind and Babe, of course, who was zapping me somehow. I was aware of it even as he was doing it and thought well, he is a ventriloquist and an impersonator so why not also a hypnotist, but just as in a dream you can know it is a dream but keep on dreaming, my knowing what Babe was up to did not affect his power to be up to it. Then his mouth came open again, and Bebb's voice came out with the lips not moving, and I remember thinking that now Babe was doing all his stunts at once. Out of his mouth Bebb's voice said, "A fiery horse with the speed of light, Antonio, a cloud of dust and a hearty Hi-yo Silver." Then there was the Lone Ranger himself.

166

I can see him now riding up over the brow of Shaw Hill in his white Stetson with his half-mask in place and a handkerchief knotted around his tanned throat. I can see the smile on his lips that would have turned Tom Mix green with envy and kept John Wayne awake at night. He was mounted on Silver with a rope at his saddle and a pair of pistols at his hips, and there was no doubt in the world who he was. He was the great champion of the down-trodden himself. He was Kemo Sabe or Faithful Friend, faithful to the task of bringing law and justice to the lawless plains at last. At his side was Tonto, and Tonto was John Turtle with his hair hanging down long and black and oily from his headband. He had his left hand cupped over his right shoulder and his right hand cupped over his left shoulder so that his fringed leather arms were crossed at his chest.

Bebb said, "I saw heaven open, and behold, a white horse, Antonio, and he that sat upon him was called Faithful and True, and in righteousness he doth judge and make war."

The Lone Ranger went galloping across the plain as tight to the saddle as though he and Silver were one, and little puffs of dust sprang up at each beat of the thundering hooves. Tonto followed along behind at an equal pace but jouncing up and down in his saddle with his elbows flopping like wings and his long hair streaming.

"Come on, Silver. Let's go, big fellow," the Lone Ranger called in that stern but reassuring baritone that had so often been a comfort to Miriam and me when we were left by ourselves in the New York apartment, and then the great Walkure shout of the Old West as he called out "Hi-yo Silver. Awa-a-ay!" and the steaming flanks gathered themselves together for a sprint up the side of a hill.

At the top of the hill the Lone Ranger and Tonto paused to scan the horizon, the masked man's gaze cutting east to west like a two-edged sword and Tonto shielding his eyes with one hand while with the other he kept knocking two of the bones around his neck together like castanets. Chicka-chock, chicka-chocka, chuck-chocka they went. The horses tossed their heads eager to resume the chase. Far off in the distance there was a railroad train winding its way through the rolling landscape. Clouds of steam trailed out from its stack, and if you strained your ears, you could just make out the wail of its whistle. Herds of buffalo scattered at its approach.

"Look, Kemo Sabe," the red man said, pointing.

The Lone Ranger said, "We haven't a moment to lose, Tonto." He had only to give the lightest touch of his heel and they were off again, heading down the far side of the hill like wind.

It is a race against death as well as against time because bound across the railroad track, directly in the path of the hurtling locomotive, is the body of a man. It is my nephew Tony Blaine, who has been trussed around from head to toe with heavy rope. His arms are pinned to his sides so that he looks as if he is in a cocoon. I can see the white clouds in his eyes as he cranes to catch sight of his approaching doom, and when our eyes meet, we both acknowledge the impossibility of my helping him in any significant way.

He says only, "I'm sorry, Tono. I'm sorry," as if it is

his fault that he is there or his fault that, to make life simpler for everybody including himself, he has not been there before this. When I ask him how he ever got in such a mess, he comes as close to shrugging his shoulders as he can, bound hand and foot, and that seems as good a way as any of saying that maybe it's not all that different from the mess he's always been in. Not so very far away now the train lets out another wail, and you can feel the faint trembling of it in the tracks.

I put my hands under his head so he won't have to keep holding it up all by himself, and his hair feels springy and matted the way it did the night he first confessed to me about himself and Sharon when by some strange reversal of roles I ended up being the one to comfort him. He has relaxed so that I can feel the full weight of his head in my hands now. It is surprisingly heavy, and I am afraid that if I should let go, his neck will break. He says, "That's some baby you've got, Tono," and as he says it, his eyes turn into x's again, and then the train is upon us, the terrible clatter and hiss and fiery brass of it, and I take the head of my namesake and cradle it against my chest just as the Lone Ranger comes galloping down the hill toward us.

There is no time to dismount, and he is hanging so far to the side from his saddle that I can't see what keeps him from falling. He has his six-shooter in his hand and is aiming it at the big hempen knot at Tony's feet. The rush of air is whipping his kerchief against his cheek, and through the eyeholes of his mask I can see his eyes narrowed against the blast of it.

Only a split second before it is too late, he fires. A silver bullet. *Zing!* The knot is shattered. The rope uncoils like a serpent. The boy springs free and heads off across the plain as the train shoots by.

I hear the voice of Bebb. He is saying, "My beloved is like a roe or a young hart. Behold, he cometh leaping upon the mountains, skipping upon the hills. He feedeth among the lilies until the day breaks and the shadows flee away."

Bebb says, "Antonio, that boy of Virgil Roebuck's, he couldn't even take his own pecker out when it come time to make a leak. All his whole life he'll have to have somebody take it out for him or just let go in his pants. When I said, 'Hope, Roebuck. Roebuck, there's always hope,' Roebuck said, 'Someday maybe he'll learn how to hold a pencil up his ass like that girl that draws the Christmas cards, and that's all the hope that boy's ever like to have.'"

Ruby Luby is lying outside in a canvas deck chair which has one bad arm. She is wearing a two-piece bathing suit, and her head is covered with tight little curls held flat to her scalp by bobby pins. She is asleep with her arms folded back over her head, and there is a pale blueish tinge to her shaved armpits. Her transistor radio is going full tilt on the ground beside her, but it has drifted to a point somewhere between a ball game and somebody singing country western through his nose.

Jimmy Bob is sitting cross-legged in the dirt not far from her feet. He has nothing on but diapers and a pair of pink rubber pants that have a few spots of what looks as if it might be dried ketchup on them. From the waist up he is the color and shape of an unbaked loaf of bread. He has a pacifier in his mouth made of the same kind of translucent brown rubber that I associate with the bathing caps nurses used to wear on the beaches of my youth, and he is chewing on it like a five cent cigar. He is playing with a snake which, like Jimmy Bob, seems to be blind. It keeps raising its head and lowering it in apparently random directions. It is a dark, nondescript-looking snake, but inside its mouth it is the color of marshmallow whip.

Not far away the Lone Ranger is squatting on his heels looking on. The sun glitters from his silver spurs, and under the dark shadow of his Stetson you cannot tell his face from his mask. In a voice so quiet and even that it comes out almost like silence, he says, "Hold it, Tonto," and John Turtle stops in his tracks. He has been crawling forward on his knees and lower arms with his butt in the air and a gummed-up looking turkey feather tucked into the back of his headband. He is naked except for a strip of rawhide around his waist and two small flaps in front and back for modesty. In his fist he has a tomahawk which he had already raised to strike at the snake when the masked man stopped him.

After several unsuccessful tries, Jimmy Bob finally locates the snake and clasps it around the neck with both hands, the rest of its long body dangling limp as a jumprope. He raises it slowly up to where he can huddle its head against him so that he and the snake end up both facing forward, check to cheek, and then at almost the same moment the snake opens its snowy mouth wide and Jimmy Bob, with his eyes going crazy, opens his mouth wide too, and they look for all the world like a pair of old drinking companions launching off into *Show Me the Way to go Home.*

Bebb says, "Antonio, there are three things which are

too wonderful for me, yea four things which I know not, the book says. There's the way of an eagle in the sky, the way of a serpent on a rock, the way of a ship in the sea, and the way of a man with a maid. Plus there's a fifth one too that's not in the book, at least not in the same part. It's the way of that man when he comes riding into the world on his silver horse with justice on one hip and mercy on the other."

He says, "Antonio, he comes like a thief in the night, like a bridegroom to the bride he's got waiting for him with flowers in her hair. You should see how they turn pale when he comes, some of them. The cheaters of widows and orphans, for one, and the lawyers they pay to make it legal. The flag-waving politicians with their hand in the till. The folks that run the sex movies and the smut stores that poison the air of the world like a open sewer. The whole miserable pack of them. He doesn't do a thing in the world to hurt them because just standing there seeing him go by is hurtful enough, all that glory galloping by they missed by being spiteful and mean. Their hearts just break against the sight of him the way waves break against a rock."

Bebb said, "But it's the others that's the real sight to see, the ones that aren't any better than they ought to be but not all that much worse either. That means all of us pretty near. He comes riding up so fast on them there's no time to put on their Sunday suit and go wait for him in the front parlor with the Scriptures laying open on the table. The midwest farmgirl that run away from home and don't have any other way to make ends meet, she's sitting all painted up on a bar stool trying to look like she knows the difference between a martini cocktail and a root beer float. The middle-age drummer that hasn't made a sale all day is stretched out on his bed in a cheap motel staring at the ceiling with the TV on. The big-time executive is bawling out his secretary for coming back from her dinner ten minutes late, and the old waitress with varicose veins is taking the weight off her feet a few minutes in the help's toilet. Of that day and hour knoweth no man, Antonio. Therefore be ye also ready, for in such an hour as ye think not the Son of Man cometh.

"Brownie," Bebb said. "That pitiful Brownie, like as not he'll be playing with himself in the bathtub or off someplace trying to make the Book of Job sound like a Mothers Day card. Sharon's twisted herself into a knot doing yogi, and I can hear Gertrude Conover explaining it out to somebody how it was to be a short order cook back in ancient Rome. Antonio, the first time they all of them hear him holler out Hi-yo Silver, the place to watch is their face."

Bebb said, "You ever looked at somebody's face sitting in the window watching for his folks to come home? Say it's gotten dark and the roads are slippery and there's been some bad accidents come over the radio. One by one he watches the headlights of cars come winding up the hill. He's got his heart in his mouth hoping this time for sure it's going to be the one to slow down and pull into the yard, but one after the other they all just keep on driving past till his face goes grey waiting for what looks like it's never going to come. Antonio, that's the face we all of us got when we're not doing anything

173

special with our face. You look at somebody the next time he's just sitting around staring into space when he doesn't know anybody's watching.

"Then finally when he's about given up hope and maybe dozed off a minute or two, he hears the back door open. He hears footsteps in the kitchen. He hears the voice out of all the voices of the world he's waiting for call out his name. Then you watch his face. Antonio, all over the world there'll be faces like that when the rider comes."

Then Bebb said, "I saw an angel standing in the sun, and he cried with a loud voice saying to all the fowls that fly in the midst of heaven, 'Come and gather yourselves together unto the supper of the great God,'" and the angel was Mr. Golden. He stood there with his queer, low-slung paunch and his porkpie hat. His withered face was lit up by his lovely girl's smile that showed his back teeth all missing. He had his arms up in the air as he spoke, and with the sun behind him they cast long shadows down over the sage-covered slope where he stood. He said, "Blessed are they which are called unto the marriage supper of the Lamb."

It was the marriage supper of Rose Trionka, only Rose coming down out of heaven this time instead of down out of the chancel of Holy Love in Houston Texas. She was vast, white, glittering, like a turreted city with pennants flying from the battlements and bunting streaming from the windows, and when she landed light as a summer cloud, the hillside blossomed all over with roses, and the Lone Ranger stepped up to take her by the fingers and lead her to the great feast.

Everybody was there. Lucille was there in a filmy,

long-waisted dress that Irene Castle might have danced the Charleston in, and my sister Miriam with a circlet of orange blossoms in her dark hair. Herman Redpath was there in a headdress of snowy egret feathers that reached to the ground and Maude Redpath in silver fox and French heels. My nephew Tony was there with Laura Fleischman, his bride, and they were dressed as they'd been at their own wedding with Tony in a rented cutaway a little skimpy at the shoulders and Laura in white tulle and sweetheart lace. Sharon's old partner at the Sharanita Shop, Anita Steen, was there in tights and ruff like Sarah Bernhardt doing Hamlet, and Metzger was there, my erstwhile neighbor at Mrs. Gunther's boarding house, the one who arranged a three-rap signal on the wall between us in case he should suddenly start having a heart attack. My dentist Darius Bildabian was there and so was my ex brother-in-law Charlie Blaine and his nurse-companion Billie Kling with her mink eyebrows and bullhorn voice.

And of course Bebb was there. He had on his maroon preaching robe with his scalp polished to a high sheen, and he came toward me bringing two people with him whom at first I didn't recognize. He told me their names, and it was only then that I saw they were my father in his World War One uniform and my Italian mother. I had just started toward them with my arms outstretched when suddenly everyone stopped talking and looked up toward the crown of the hillside where we were all gathered.

The Lone Ranger and Rose Trionka were standing against the sky. The Lone Ranger reached out and raised the veil from his bride's face. Then he reached up and

175

took hold of the corner of his mask. When he pulled it off at last, the light was so overwhelming that for a few moments, like Emily Dickinson "I could not see to see."

When I could see again, it was Babe I saw—Babe the ufologist, ventriloquist, hypnotist, impersonator, in his T-shirt and jumbo shorts but dozing now in the afternoon sun, slumped over at the middle like a grain sack with his mouth ajar. He was a trickster and a slanderer, and by his own admission he believed the Gospel was just a way of putting things to people who weren't ready yet for the headier truths of Ufology. But insofar as he was the creator of my dream, I think he created it because with part of himself he would have liked to dream it too. I suspect that for Babe not believing may sometimes have been hard as Bebb said believing was.

Anyway, when he woke up and fixed me with those saucer-spotting eyes again, he said, "I've got to make a living same as everybody else, Antonio. I usually get ten bucks for a consultation and five for a life-ray treatment, but seeing as you're kin, I'll make it ten even," and the way he said it, sitting there so fat and crooked and unabashed, I could see how if you didn't have anything else handy to put your faith in, you might be tempted, like Brownie, to put it in him.

CHAPTER TWELVE

A NUMBER OF THINGS happened elsewhere while I was having my consultation with Babe. Callaway found himself locked out of his room and his extra pair of pants, his beautiful shirts, his Agway cap, and everything he owned thrown into a heap in the place where the ice machine and the trash bin were. Gertrude Conover wanted to force a showdown with the manager then and there, but Callaway dissuaded her. He made a long speech which Sharon said even she had a hard time understanding, but apparently he got very excited in the course of it and at one point made a gesture of such violence that it knocked Brownie's glasses off and badly

177

cracked one of the lenses. The result of the speech was that Gertrude Conover insisted they find another motel for Callaway and Brownie both, and the four of them set out in the Continental, dropping Sharon off at Babe's on the way because she saw it as an opportunity to wash her hair while nobody else was waiting for the can. She was on her way upstairs to do it when she nearly fell over Bert, who was sitting on the top step in her saddle shoes and bobby socks with her flyswatter on one side of her and a suitcase held together with clothesline on the other. She told Sharon she had been waiting for her and had a place she wanted to take her to and some things she wanted to show her. So Sharon put off the shampoo, and carrying the suitcase between them they walked up into the pine woods where Babe and I had jogged and kept going till they reached the place where the little collection of Stredwig gravestones stood among rusted out Sterno cans and the remains of a fence. The largest of the stones lay flat on the ground, the inscription long since garbled by weather, and while Babe and I were journeying into the future on Shaw Hill, Bert and Sharon sat down on the stone, the suitcase across Bert's knees, and started out on a journey of their own. The suitcase was of course the one that Bert had first pointed out in the little varnished room at the top of the back stairs, the one where she said she kept her treasures.

Apparently Bert did very little talking at first, and when I think of the scene, I think of the place in *Hamlet* where Polonius quizzes Ophelia on what the Prince said to her, and Ophelia answers with the speech in which she describes no words he spoke but goes on in some detail about what he did with his hands, arms, shoulders, eyes, face, to which Polonius then replies, "This is the very ecstasy of love." That's the way I see Bert sitting there among the graves beside Sharon, not saying much but moving the way clouds move, which is to say so slowly and subtly you can hardly see what is happening until little by little it has happened. As one by one she pulls her treasures out of the suitcase on her lap, small things go on in her face that make big differences. The forehead puckers, the eyes go puddled and dark, the cheeks melt in places like snow. I see her whole bulk shifting—a saddle shoe toeing slightly inward, a grey curl trembling, as she hands things to Sharon in whatever order she happens to come on them.

There were photographs with no shadows in them—a woman walking away from a square car with a paper bag in her arms, two men in straw hats sitting in rockers with water behind them, a woman with the top of her head gone. Once in a while Bert would say something. "This is the summer I turned nineteen?" she said. She said, "That's the one they called Fiddling Sam? Played at our senior hop?" She said, "When she took sick the last time, they forgot and left her in the hammock the whole day. She was all over honeybees when they found her? All that cologne, they thought she was a rosebush?" She said, "That's your daddy?" and Sharon said to me, "When she was handing me the ones of Bip, she pressed her lips together and hummed little tunes." There was Bip in knickers. There was Bip in an open roadster holding up a copy of Scripture in each hand. There was Bip with his face so faded out his features looked like bird tracks in the snow.

She said, "I said, 'Bert, you want me to read this?' She

179

took it out of the envelope and spread it out on my lap for me. You'd have thought I was a big doll. She put her hand on my head and bent it like a doll's so I'd read it."

Sharon read it to me. It said, " 'My own sweet honey love, I was in tears for you last night. What's it mean when a man's heart's so full he cries tears? If God is love like the book says, then the love God is is tears because that's what it is for me most of the time we're apart and I have to pretend like I don't care. Every time he says you two this, you two that, my heart skips a beat. I'll be there the same time tomorrow anyhow no matter if you come or not. If God is love there's no love doesn't have some God in it along with all the rest it's got in it too. You are my love and tears both, and there's nothing God doesn't wash whiter than snow in the end though it makes his love cry tears too. Sweet dreams to my own sweet honey love.' " Bert's face slowly tumbled together like clouds, a stray wisp disappearing into the sky. Her nostrils swelled out with the tune she was humming, Sharon's head bent like a doll's beside her.

Sharon said, "I said, 'Jesus, Bert. That's a moonflop.' It was wrapped up in pink tissue with a rubber band and it was about the same shape as a moonflop only littler. It was a round piece of hard clay with this little bit of a hand-print pressed into it like they do in grade school. It had a hole in it to hang it up, and it had a name scratched in with a match it looked like. Bert said, 'He went and stole it for me?' and I said, 'You're asking me, Bert?' She said, 'I'm telling you, honey.' "

Sharon said, "She said Bip went and stole it away from Luce and mailed it to her. She said she never saw him after he married Luce and moved to Knoxville but sometimes he'd write her a line or two. She's got them all saved. Sometimes all he wrote were words out of Scripture. He'd write her things like 'Damsel, I say unto thee arise' and 'Let him who is without sin cast the first stone' and 'Lo I am with you alway, even unto the end of the world.' "

Sharon said, "She had things in there too she'd found laying around the house from when he was growing up in it. There was his lunch pail he took to school with him that's got his name still scratched on the lid and a piece of scorecard where he'd got Babe Ruth to sign his name on it when he came through Spartanburg once. She had a diary in there he'd kept for a while. It was lots of it just how he laid out five cents for phosphate or fishline or something and how he took in a quarter drawing stove wood in his wagon, but there were places he'd list off his sins for the week. He wrote he copied off of Emma Missildine's paper, and he and his buddy caught them a bullfrog and played toss with it till one of its legs came off. He put down the times he used bad language and things like *sassed Mama* with a number after it. Bert said there were plenty of good deeds he could have put down too, but I told her when you do a good deed, you're not even supposed to act like you notice it."

"He raised a sigh so piteous and profound," Ophelia says, "as it did seem to shatter all his bulk," and I picture Bert's shattered bulk as she turns to Sharon there among the fallen stones and hands her a snapshot of herself as she was before her features started huddling together for protection and she put on all that flesh—a flapper with her hair flat to her cheeks and her stockings rolled below the knee. She and Babe are sitting side by

181

side on some porch steps and behind them a woman in a long skirt with her head and shoulders lost in the shadow of the porch roof. She says, "That's Babe's mother?" She says, "That's the year I lost my baby?" and Sharon says, "I didn't know you and Babe had a baby," and Bert says, "It wasn't Babe's baby I had." Then that profound and piteous sigh that shook the grey curls, the fat arms, cracked the face down the middle in an ecstasy of love.

Sharon said, "I mean Jesus, Bopper, what could I say? 'Whose baby?' I said, 'Take it easy, Bert.' She had all that stuff out of the grip scattered around her and more stuff still to go, and she was sitting there making that little sound she makes to the chickens heekie, heekie, heekie. I just said, 'Take it easy, Bert,' and after a while it came out piece by piece like she was counting out money.

"Bip did it again," Sharon said. "He and Luce weren't married yet, but Babe and Bert were. She said there was a time they were both of them courting her together, and for a while she couldn't choose between them, but she fixed on Babe finally because Bip was already starting to get into selling Bibles and Babe was home more. She and Babe got married and lived with the mother, and Bip would come home weekends some. She and Bip would go off together berrying. Babe got sun-rash so he didn't go, just the two of them with their pails up there on that hill where Babe says the UFOs are supposed to land. I guess that's why he wants them to land up there so he'll have something else to remember that hill by. When Bert was telling about it, she was like a saucer herself getting ready to land. She'd tell about it as far as the hill, and then just when she was going to come out with it, she'd make that chicken noise again and shy off. And pulling more stuff out of the grip the whole time. Like those notes made up out of Scripture that sometimes didn't even have Bip's name signed on them. Sometimes they'd just be words of hymns like 'The night is dark and I am far from home' and 'I need thee every hour.' "

Sharon said, "She finally made a three point landing and told it like it was. She said she and Bip made it up there in the berrybushes and the clouds while Babe was back home taking care of his sun-rash. It just about killed them both afterwards, the shame of it, and they vowed they'd never let it happen again. Bip went and married Luce to make sure it wouldn't. Then Bert found out she was going to have Bip's baby. She tried to make out at first like it was Babe's, but Babe knew it wasn't and finally wormed it out of her whose it really was. He had his suspicions from the start. She said he carried on so it almost made her lose her baby. Babe said when the baby was born he wouldn't have it in his house, and he went to Knoxville and raised hell with Bip over it. There was this terrible row, the two of them rolling around on the floor pounding each other to pieces and poor Luce there watching. She was pregnant with the baby that later on died so there were these two women both of them pregnant by Bip, and Bert says part of what sent Babe clear out of his head was he couldn't make anybody pregnant himself. It seems like he was the twin that got the hair and Bip was the twin that got the balls, and he all but killed Bip, beating on his head till his eyes were so swelled up one of them never did work right again from then on. Jesus, Bopper, the way she sat there telling it all with her treasures scattered around her like a picnic and the sweat rolling down out of her wig."

It was later that night that Sharon told me and in the kitchen, of course, that room that has always been the Oval Office of my life, the place where the great crises sizzle and snap like bacon, where most of my major decisions have been made like breakfast. The events of the day had been such that we were divided into two hostile camps by then, and everybody except Sharon and me was trying to get some sleep before what was bound to be some kind of showdown the next day. The only light was the little one over the stove, and it was both very peaceful and very charged in there with the fireflies twinkling outside like enemy campfires. We were sitting at the kitchen table, and Sharon was looking down at it, tracing circles with her finger where the evening before Babe's black coffee and black cake had made circles.

"Poor Bert," she said. "She lost Bip and Babe both. She lost her hair. She lost her baby. It was a girl."

"Died?" I said.

She said, "Adopted. Babe swore he'd kill it if she ever brought it home."

I said, "Has she ever seen it since?" and she said, "She's seen it."

"Bip's own flesh and blood floating around somewhere," I said. "It gives you a queer feeling."

"Queer as hell," she said.

I suppose it was the lateness of the hour that had slowed me down, not to mention the lingering effect of the life-ray and the anticipation of bloodshed to come, but up until then I had thought it was Bert she was mainly telling me about. Then she glanced up from her circles with a look on her face that I don't think I had ever seen there before. Up till then the only opening I had known into the secret of her face was that sudden flare of a smile she had, but as I looked at her now, her whole face was flickering with secret like a candle though there wasn't a smile within miles—just those guilty eyes, that somber mouth—and I said, "Who adopted Bert's baby anyway?" and she said, "I'll give you three guesses," and it was only then that in the balloon above my head the lightbulb came on the full five hundred watts worth at last, and I said, "Jesus Christ. I don't believe it."

She said, "You better believe it, Bopper. That's the truth of it," and I said, "You know, it's a funny thing, but there's someplace in me where I've always known it was." She said, "Put her there then. I've always known it was too," her hand coming at me over the white table. Then right there in the Oval Office with everybody else asleep I shook hands with the flesh and blood of Leo Bebb and for the first time in my life knew for sure that that was who I was shaking hands with and knew a lot of other things besides.

The present is always up for grabs, of course, and the future, who knows, but at least the past you think you've got salted away where neither moth nor rust doth corrupt nor thieves break through and steal. Then the first thing you know, the past starts playing tricks on you too. Like coffee that's spilled on page one hundred and stains its way back through page twenty-five, the revelation of Sharon's true identity—the strawberry mark on the left shoulder, the coronet on the baby blanket— changed the shape of events I'd thought were safe long since. I think of that evening barbecue at the Redpath Ranch when I proposed to her, for instance—how as she came walking toward me through the firelit Indians with her arm in a sling and wearing a moonlight-colored dress, Bebb appeared behind me and softly spoke words into my ear to the effect that she was mine for the taking. What he was inviting me to take, of course, was not just the apple of his eye but the flesh of his flesh, the breath of his life, and it was not until all those long years later that I understood she was more precious to him than he could possibly tell without impossibly telling at the same time the whole unseemly tale of his dalliance with Bert among the clouds and berry bushes and the terrible time in Knoxville, Tennessee, when those two roly-polies tried to destroy each other at the feet of poor, pregnant Lucille.

And I think of the last time Bebb and Sharon ever saw each other. It was in the basement of the storage warehouse where Bebb was hiding out from his enemies, and the two of them were sitting side by side in front of a scene Mr. Golden had painted on the wall that showed some feather-duster palm trees against a blue sky with a flock of birds flying across it like black checkmarks. Sharon had her head on Bebb's shoulder, and they both of them had a kind of dreaming look in their eyes as though they were looking at a sunset. The truth of it was that what Bebb was looking at was the knowledge that this was the last chance he'd ever get to tell her who he was and who she was and that he was never going to tell her.

And Lucille and Bert, Bebb's two great loves—in the new light I saw them both in new ways too. Lucille sits in front of the color TV with her dark glasses on and a Tropicana in her hand; and the TV, the dark glasses, the Tropicanas, all three, are what she uses to hide behind from everybody including herself. Why did she develop her taste for gin and orange juice? Why did what happened to her baby happen? Why did Bebb marry her in the first place? She drops her lower jaw in what it takes an expert to spot as a smile. "You tell me," she says with that Foster Grant blank where her eyes ought to be. She looks like someone watching a total eclipse of the sun.

The first time we meet her, Bert says, "Has he passed?" Passed out, passed through? She is holding Babe's charred shoulderpads in her hand. Rain falls on the Uforium roof. Her face is the moon, and when I answer that he has passed indeed, I watch my answer make its historic landing there, and I think at the time that it's only Babe's brother we are talking about, a man it's been years since she thought of last.

Thus Bert's graveyard disclosures as Sharon reported them to me late that night cast light on many things, but nowhere was the light they cast more illuminating than on the garish event that had taken place only a few hours earlier to make of that day the Hallowe'en of my life, as I look back on it, with false faces falling off and the truth beneath the white sheet turning out to be a truth to make the hair stand on end.

It was after I had had my life-ray treatment on Shaw Hill and after poor Bert had spilled the beans to Sharon in the woods. Around five or so Gertrude Conover came back from her tour with Brownie and Callaway bearing the news that there wasn't a motel to be found that would take them in. She bore the news also that Callaway had had another nosebleed. The two facts were not, in her estimation, unrelated. Theosophically speaking, she said, no facts were unrelated. The motel keepers' intransigence, suggesting that Babe's slanders had spread like the plague, was the problem, she said; and the nosebleed, suggesting what it always suggested, pointed to a solution. The solution was that we should seek out Bebb. Having gotten us to Poinsett in the first place, he was the logical one for us to turn to for help. There was no question in her mind where we should look for him. She had the address in her pocket where she had put it when Ruby Luby gave it to her at the well baby clinic. It was Lola's Trailer Court. She said that since in his present incarnation Bebb was only a year or so old, it might take something to jog his memory about who we were and what we needed him for, and luckily, anticipating some such eventuality, she had brought along a relic that should do the trick nicely. It was Bebb's maroon preaching robe, the same one that he had led his famous march on Nassau Hall in, and although Jimmy Bob would not be able to see it, of course, she felt that just its presence should be sufficient. Babe was not around when we left, only Bert, resting upstairs, and Sharon slipped a note under her door telling her where we were going just in case she needed us.

In my normal state of mind I don't think I could have set off on such a crackpot errand without cracking up in the process somehow myself, but by then I was not in my normal state of mind. Beginning, I suppose, with the experience of thinking that I'd seen Bebb in the Library of Congress reading room and proceeding from there to the moonrocks, the transistorized teeth, Jimmy Bob, the life-ray, the Lone Ranger, I had moved step by step to a kind of panicky openness to almost any possibility, which I suspect must be, if not the same thing as what people like Bebb would call faith, at least its kissing cousin. Sharon and I, Callaway and Brownie and Gertrude Conover, there we were, all five of us, piled into the Continental with the maroon preaching robe folded up in Gertrude Conover's lap like the flag they give a soldier's widow, bound for a trailer-court interview with the reincarnation of a dead evangelist, and although I thought even at the time that it was folly to believe anything could come of it, I thought too that it would be a greater folly still to believe that nothing possibly could. In a world where we are often closer to the truth in dreams than anywhere else, who is to say what is possible and not possible, true and not true, any more than in dreams you can say it? Callaway drove with Brownie beside him, the two ladies and I in back, and I thought of Gideon and Barak and Samson and all those others who are said to have spent their lives dreaming of a homeland which they had had only a glimpse of from afar and not all that clear a glimpse either. I mentioned them to Brownie as we set off just to see what he would say, and I remember him still as he turned to look at me over the back of his seat through his cracked lenses and said, "They were the great heroes of the faith, dear, but they died still guessing just like the rest of us."

Lola's Trailer Court was a raw, jerrybuilt-looking place right off the main road across from a drive-in movie. The trailers didn't seem to have been parked in any special order but just abandoned at various angles around a one story cinderblock building with a Kwik Wash and a coke machine and an office where presumably Lola herself did business. There were some lines strung up with wash hanging on them. There were some trash-filled oil drums. There was a man with a bottle wrapped in a brown paper bag who pointed out where the Lubys' trailer was. It was out on the edge of things, and we moved our car to a place nearer to it where there was a stand of pines and some bird-spattered picnic tables.

It had turned overcast and much hotter since the freshness of the morning, and the light was hazy and dim with a sense of thunder in the air. Gertrude Conover looked pale and older than usual standing by the picnic tables with the robe over her arm. Her hair had lost much of its blue and didn't have the same bounce to it. Her upper lip was moist with perspiration. Her spirit, however, remained undampened as she explained her strategy to us. It was not uncomplicated. We would all go to the trailer, she said, but only she would go in, because she didn't want to scare the Lubys out of their wits right at the start and there wouldn't be room for all five of us anyway. The rest of us would wait outside where the combined force of our karmic fields would, even through the trailer walls, start stirring in Jimmy Bob memories of the life he had once lived among us. It was important, Gertrude Conover said, not to stir them too much or too soon because she wouldn't want the child to reveal anything in front of his parents that might alarm them or lead them to suspect that there was anything unusual about him. "He will have a hard enough time in that family as it is, poor thing," she said, and for the same reason she would not bring the maroon preaching robe in with her because with all its rich Bebbsian associations she expected it to open the door wide in him that our combined karma would have barely pushed ajar. We would leave it in the car instead, she said, and after spreading it out over the front seat, to increase its power to awaken Jimmy Bob, she pinned to it one of the flyers that had been passed out during the same famous march in Princeton. Just to make sure. "Ban the Bomb not Bebb" it said, in reference to the University's eviction of the love feasts from Alexander Hall, and there was a head-and-shoulders mug shot of Bebb with his eyes bugged out and his mouth clamped shut that Sharon said made him look as if he was having his temperature taken rectally.

The trick, Gertrude Conover said, would be to get the baby to the robe without his parents. She said, "I will explain that we were just passing by and happened to recognize the address she gave us. She will remember how I took an interest in the child at the clinic, and I will tell her I wanted to see him again before we left. Maybe I will tell her I have some little present for him in the car, or maybe I will ask to take him for a stroll in his pushcart while the rest of you stay by the trailer to distract her. Well, I will depend on the inspiration of the moment. We will see what we will see."

Sharon said, "How do you figure he's going to be able to help us, Gertrude Conover? He can't see the hand in front of his face and he probably doesn't have ten words he can say together in a row."

Gertrude Conover said, "Who knows what he can see? As for helping us, he has helped us already. He has given us a point to rally around when we're all at sea about what to do next. My dear, he has given us hope."

Brownie said, "A little child shall lead them, the prophet says. The trouble is where is there to lead us to when we're all lost in the dark together?"

He said, "It's the blind leading the blind, dear. We can't any of us see much more than the hand in front of our face. Nobody knows for sure there even is a hand." I could hear in his speech that he must have taken a little something before we left, and I wondered if Mother was home still and how the new set of teeth was coming along. I wondered how rough a time he was having of it now that the Babe he so admired had turned against the Callaway he so loved and how he would ever be able to choose between them if the time ever came when he had to choose. Gertrude Conover led the way to the Luby's trailer, and the rest of us followed along in single file. The bodies of the trailers were silvery and dim in the fading light. We could have been threading our way through wrecks at the bottom of the sea.

It was Ruby Luby who answered Gertrude Conover's knock. There was a smell of frying food as she stood in the doorway with children peering out from behind her skinny legs. Gertrude Conover did the talking while the rest of us hovered around in the background radiating karma. In a few moments they disappeared into the trailer together, and the door closed behind them. Then Callaway had a recurrence of his nosebleed.

It wasn't one of his worst ones by a long shot, but it was enough to keep us occupied while we waited for Gertrude Conover to reappear with Jimmy Bob. Brownie walked back to the coke machine and returned with a cold bottle which Callaway pressed to his upper lip while at the same time somehow holding the handkerchief in place. I wondered how much he understood of what we were there to accomplish and whether Gertrude Conover had ever explained to him her theory about his nosebleeds, and then finally the door opened again and Gertrude Conover came out with Jimmy Bob in her arms. Ruby came out too in some kind of Sears Roebuck sunsuit. Then a T-shirted man I took to be her husband came with a beer belly swelling out over his belt and a disagreeable face with the upper lip caved in. They stood there on the steps for a moment as though posing for a photograph, and then suddenly Gertrude Conover pointed out over our heads to where we had left the car. "Good God," she said, and my first thought was that it was part of her ruse for getting Jimmy Bob to the preaching gown. It was not.

It was Bert. Even at a distance and through the dwindling light, I could recognise the grey curls, the shapeless bulk. Like the time at the hen house, there was something violent going on though at first it was hard to see what. She was standing at the car with her back to us. Her shoulders were heaving, and you could tell she was doing something that required great strength and great concentration. She could have been a medieval executioner gutting a felon. There was a wrenching, rasping sound. She was getting her back into it. Something gave way, and for a moment she almost lost her balance. Then one arm shot up, and something flew glittering through the air. It was the side-view mirror that had been torn from its socket. She did the same thing in half the time with the aerial. She took some weapon I could not identify and like Casey at the bat swung it full force against one of the side windows. There was a sound of shattering glass. She flung the door open and the horn blared as she must have hit it leaning in. Something flashed red, then redder and bigger as she held it out wide. It was Bebb's robe with his picture pinned to it, and eyeball to eyeball they must have stared at each other for a moment or two as I pulled myself together sufficiently to start running toward them. Even as I ran, the most furious part of the attack took place.

It must have been recognizing the picture and seeing whose robe it was that triggered it. She ripped at the robe, yanked it, punched it, for all I know took it between her teeth and gnawed at it. She threw it to the ground and leaped on it. Like Oliver Hardy demolishing a Model T, she jumped up and down on it with her arms flung wide, her head bent low, her legs pumping. There was terror in it and comedy in it and a deep, twilit silence in it that heightened them both because from where I was anyway she made no more noise in her rage than she would have made in a dream about rage. Then I reached her and there took place the final falling apart into two of things, the refusal of things to stay put, stay simple and unitary and true enough for a man to put his trust in and get his bearings by. I grabbed her by the shoulders and spun her around, and it was only then that I saw that the person standing there in that tent of a dress with the massive grey wig knocked crooked was not Bert at all. It was Babe.

It was Babe looking the way he had that night by the refrigerator with the dead hen in his hand, Babe with his face shattered like the window of the car and put back together by a creature from outer space who'd never seen more than a rough diagram of a face. He gave me one wild, searching look and then broke loose from my grasp. Clutching his dress in a knot at his groin, he ran back toward the trailer as best he could where the others were still standing too flabbergasted to move. Then back toward me again. Then he stopped dead in his tracks for a moment, his bare legs milky pale beneath his trussed-up skirts.

"Laverne!" he shouted in a windy, faraway voice like the voice a child hears calling him home when evening comes, and with all the other thoughts running through my mind, the one that outran the lot was the thought that this was Brownie's moment of truth. Did he go to Babe or did he stay with the others by the trailer? Gertrude Conover was the only one of them left on the trailer steps. She stood in the open doorway with Jimmy Bob in her arms. He was a big baby, and she was standing at an awkward angle so she could support part of his weight on her hip. He had one hand in the air in front of him, the palm facing out. Though he was straddling her hip, his face was turned in the same direction hers was. If he hadn't been blind, you would have said he was gazing toward Babe like the rest of us, maybe even signaling to him.

Once more the sound of Brownie's name went drifting through the air, and this time Brownie responded. I can see him still as he moved slowly away from his friends. I couldn't see his face from that distance, but if I could, I would have looked the other way. I suppose it was Mother who was calling him—Mother in drag, with her curls knocked cockeyed, the sweat rolling down. All around us the dim hulks of the trailers glimmered. By the mutilated Continental, the red robe lay stamped into the red dust and what was left of Bebb's face on the flyer goggled up at the darkening sky. In the arms of Gertrude Conover, fluttering his small, flat eyes, maybe Jimmy Bob said something, but if so, nobody heard him.

Nobody did anything. We all just watched as Babe and Brownie moved off through the dusk together with their arms around each other somehow, holding each other up. They headed for the picnic tables. They disappeared into the pines where the branches swallowed them up, babes in the woods. I was the only one who had been close enough to see who the car's attacker really was, but I didn't want to say anything about it in front of the Lubys, and when I finally did say it on the ride home with Callaway at the wheel—his dignity intact despite the raw, twisted scars where the aerial and side-view mirror had been and the cobweb-shattered window —I don't think they really believed it. Even I didn't entirely believe it.

As soon as we got home, the four of us filed upstairs to Bert's bedroom, a stunned and silent deputation, and there she was, as fast asleep as when Sharon had left her note. She was lying in bed bald as an egg with her suitcase on the floor beside her. The clothesline was tied back around it. We did not wake her.

There was so much to say that nobody had the energy to try to start saying it. Gertrude Conover was the one who seemed the most done in. In addition to everything else, there had been her long, unsuccessful search for a new motel for Callaway, and she looked exhausted. Her walk was unsteady, her seams crookeder than usual, more loose hairpins dangling. Nevertheless, before retiring for the night, she pulled herself together and made a small speech.

She said, "Well, it was a disappointment. Why pretend it wasn't? I am getting old. I am old as the hills already. I know my theosophy must seem far-fetched and dotty to you. There are times when it seems far-fetched and dotty to me. Do I remember my past lives, or do I just dream them up? Maybe the past is always something you just dream up. Who can be sure of anything when you come right down to it? I had such high hopes. A little touch of Leo in the night. I had hoped that Jimmy Bob might give some sign. Well, he didn't. It has left me feeling very blue. I feel very blue and old and dumb.

"And yet," she said, her hand on the varnished bannister, "Thank your stars there is always *and yet*. This side of Paradise, perhaps it is the best you can hope for. Jimmy Bob gave no sign, but think of it this way. If it weren't for him, what happened this evening would never have happened. If it weren't for him, we would have gone on thinking that it was poor Bert playing Yahoo tricks all these years when all along it was Babe. I don't believe for a moment this was the first time. Obviously the man is mad. So maybe what happened this evening was itself the sign. And what didn't happen was a sign too. It was a sign saying not to look for miraculous signs because we wouldn't see them even if they were served up to us on a silver platter. My dear, everything that happens is absolutely seething with miracle, and who sees it? Who even wants to see it most of the time?

Life is confusing enough as it is."

She went about half way up the stairs, her slip show-ing. The bannister creaked as she leaned on it. Then she turned once again and looked back at us over her shoul-der. "One more thing," she said, "and then I will shut up and go to bed. It is just this. I held him in my arms again. You don't have to be a theosophist to see what a wretched time he is going to have growing up in that family. You should have seen the inside of that trailer, and I shudder when I think of the meanness and ignor-ance in the face of his father. Leo Bebb has always had frightful luck with his fathers. But when I held him in my arms, all those sad things seemed to melt away. All the things that menace him seemed to draw back like wild animals from a fire, and all the things that menace me too. I could feel it in my bones, and I know he could feel it too. He laid his little head against me, and you can call it dotty if you want, but for a moment I believe even death itself drew back. There was nothing in heaven or earth that could hurt us. I believe that for a moment we achieved cosmic consciousness, my dear old friend and I, and not even death and all his minions could touch us with a ten-foot pole."

She said, "I am going up now. It has been the longest day of my life. When I'm finished with the bathroom, I will leave the door open. Sweet dreams."

I asked Sharon two questions before we finally went upstairs ourselves. The first question was what had hap-pened between her and Bert when she first found out she was her mother, and Sharon said, "It wasn't like we made a big fuss over each other or anything like that. It was more like it made us strangers all over again. I could feel my face go all frozen and queer on me. Neither of us said much. What can you say? She had all that stuff to put back in her grip again, and I helped her. We lugged it home together through the trees. I didn't kiss her even, or her me. It wasn't till I looked in on her before we left for Lola's that I kissed her just once on top of her old bald head, and she didn't even know it. I could have been kissing Bip the way it felt. It was like when I used to kiss Bip on top of his old bald head the same way."

The second question was why, when she'd found the truth out that afternoon, she'd waited till then to tell me about it, and she said, "I used to lay awake nights wondering who my real folks were, and when I finally found out, it was like I wanted to just keep it to myself a while. For a few hours there wasn't anybody in the whole world that knew Bip was my father and Bert was my mother except me and Bert. Not even you, Bopper. I guess it was the closest I ever got to a family reunion."

Then she said, "She gave me this out of her grip the last thing she did before she closed it up again. She told me it proved who I was in case I ever had to prove it, and I could have it if I'd keep it safe somewhere and never lose it."

It was written in Bebb's hand on the back of a Light of Truth Bible Company order blank, and it said, "Dear One, I went and picked her up today where you said and brought her home to Luce. Luce was laying on the sofa tuned in to Major Bowes on the wireless. She's been listening to that thing day in day out for weeks. I guess it takes her mind off things. When I set the baby alongside her on the sofa, she didn't even look like she noticed, so for a while there I just about died. Finally she reached down and poked the blanket back with one finger so she could see what it looked like inside, and there was that pitiful little bundled-up thing watching her with those big eyes she's got on her like she knows the secret of life. It was like I'd given her her own baby back she'd lost. She picked it up and cuddled it against her, and things started in to happen all over her whole face you could tell she's got a chance again now to join the human race. Before, she was a goner if I ever saw one the way she was just laying there day after day on the sofa with the wireless going. So you see you've done the right thing letting her take the baby.

"Bert, my ways are not thy ways, saith the Lord. You'd think that baby was the love of God incarnate the change she's made for good in Luce's poor broken heart always thinking back on the awful thing she did when she was out of her head with drink. You don't ever have to worry again our baby won't have all the love a baby ever had in this world. Luce has fixed on giving her the name of Sharon. I guess you know the name I would have given her, but it's all the same anyway.

"Bert, let's never forget what was pure and good that we had between us, and let's never remember more than we can help it what was shameful. The judgment upon us is we'll never set eyes on each other again this side of glory, and Sharon she'll never know who we truly are to her till then either. It's not the way we either one of us would have ever picked, but there's not any way on this earth doesn't lead to the throne of grace in the end if that's where you've got your heart set on going. Farewell, my own dear heart. I won't ever forget. Remember me in your prayers the same as I'll always remember you, and remember our little one.

Leo Bebb."

CHAPTER THIRTEEN

SINCE BABE still had her wig, wherever he was, Bert had
to make do the next morning with a hat. It was an old-
lady straw-colored straw hat with pale blue and green
paper roses at the brim, and she came down to make
breakfast wearing it and a sleazy, flowery dressing gown
to go with it that fluttered when she moved, a whole
bank of flowers nodding in the breeze. Sharon said later
she looked like a garden party at the funny farm, but if
so, one of the great garden parties, her face more at rest
than I'd ever seen it, blooming almost, the features no
longer so crowded, the forehead unpuckered. Of course
it was the first time I'd ever seen her as Bebb's dark and

secret love, more even than Lucille and Gertrude Conover the real love of his life, I suppose, not to mention the mother of Sharon, the grandmother of my children whom she didn't even know existed, my own mother-in-law. All of it came at me full force for the first time as she moved around like late spring putting breakfast together. She said, "Where's Babe?"

It was her only question up to that point, the day so drowsy still with early sun, so unopened, that there'd been no time yet for other questions. It was the one I dreaded. I didn't want to tell her about Lola's Trailer Court and went at it in such an oblique way it's a wonder she knew what I was talking about. I told her about parking the Continental by the bird-spattered picnic tables and how the trailers looked like sunken ships. I slipped it in about somebody's appearing out of the pines while we were waiting for Gertrude Conover to come out. I alluded to his doing something strange and violent to the Continental. I mentioned that in the dwindling light it was hard to make out just who he was, and then in that little toy voice she said, "It was Babe?" and I didn't have to answer for her to know the answer.

She said, "He have on my wig and things?" and when I nodded, she said, "I always knew it was Babe."

I said, "Why didn't you tell people it was Babe for God's sake?" and she said, "Who'd believe a Stredwig?" So all in a moment I saw her not just as Bebb's dark and secret love but as the bearer of yet another secret of her own—that year after year she had sat there bald as an egg while Babe went out in her grey curls smashing things, and that swatting flies and smoking cigarettes she had known year after year that he was doing it.

It was my turn to ask the questions then, and her answers came with question marks after them the way everything she said came with a question mark after it to indicate that if you found what she had to say not to your liking for any reason, you were free to change it to anything you liked better just as Babe was free to dress up in her clothes and Bebb was free to adopt their baby and never tell her who she was for fear the shame of it might be too much for them all. "Who'd believe a Stredwig?" she said, as if she wouldn't be apt to believe herself even unless you gave her special leave and encouragement. There she was, known for the first time for who she truly was and what she truly knew, yet that didn't seem to shield her any better from the world than her sleazy wrapper or paper roses shielded her. Her little question-answers came pitter-pattering out.

"He's not to blame?" she said. "After what I did, I had it coming? It was a shameful thing? Leo and me we never planned it to happen like it did. It just happened a little at a time up to where one day Leo said, 'Bert, I don't even know my right name any more. I don't even know Jesus any more. You're the only one I know for sure out of the whole world, Bert. You're the only one I need to know.' It's scary, that kind of loving? It gives you the power of life and death?"

I thought of Bebb as she quoted him, how part of what he treasured inside that fat, buttoned-up face was the memory of the time he no longer knew the name of Jesus, how part of what he had bared in Miami Beach like a wound for the flummoxed children somehow to heal must have been the shame of it.

Bert broke six white eggs into a white bowl and beat

them with a fork, her roses trembling. She said, "Every year there'd be windows broken? There'd be flower-beds stomped and trash cans pushed over. A privy'd catch fire? A chicken's neck wrung? My poor Heekie. I always could tell by when my wig was gone. Babe's smart? He knows I'd sooner die than go out bald-headed. That way there wasn't ever a chance of two of me showing up at the same time?"

She said, "Folks in Points think a lot of Babe but they're scared too? Him and his life-ray? Nobody ever did anything if they saw crazy old Bert doing crazy things come sundown. They no more mentioned it to him than if I was a harelip he had or a crooked leg. I didn't either? I never once said, 'Babe how come you're doing it?' I couldn't shame him, saying it out like that."

"Why did he do it, Bert?" I said.

She said, "What man would ever look twice at a woman that knocks down pea-fences at night? Children poke each other when they see me. I don't go downstreet any more hardly, except the dentist? He wants me like one of his moonrocks. He does it so nobody'll get too close for fear of moongerms. That's why?"

She said, "Sometimes I talk to him in my mind? I say, 'Babe, you ever going to be done revenging yourself?' He says, 'Bert, I'm not revenging anymore.' He says, 'I'm keeping you safe, Bert. I'm making it so there won't ever anybody get at and hurt you again.' "

"Jesus," Sharon said. She said, "You're going to get the hell out of here, Bert. You're going to pack your things and come home with us. You tell her, Bopper. She can't stay here with that sonofabitch," and I remember still Bert's face wilting as she said it.

205

She said, "He was taking a big chance doing it there at Lola's in broad daylight?"

I said, "Bip used to take big chances. Maybe it's in their blood."

"The hell you say," Sharon said. "Bip took chances there was a god in heaven and angels on earth with gold and silver faces on them. The only chances Babe ever took was nobody'd catch him out a liar—all that shit about going to the moon."

Bert said, "That's not shit, honey? He's told me about the moon till it's like I've been there my ownself?"

The coffee was perking and upstairs you could hear Gertrude Conover and Callaway moving around. In the grey light from the window, Bert's face became the moon she was thinking about. She said, "Babe says it's all over little round stones like goat turds. It's just miles and miles of goat turds far as the eye can see. Babe says it's got this awful odor to it too? He says it's so strong it seeps in through your space helmet? He says the whole moon smells like where it needs mopping up around the toilet, all musty and sharp like stale wee."

"The other planets have it too?" she said. "Babe says the creatures live on them have to keep plugs in their noses it's so bad."

"That's where they're going to spacelift us to?" Sharon said. "Jesus."

Bert said, "They've got shots against death there, honey?"

"Hot damn," Sharon said.

I said, "You believe it, Bert?" and her answer was as uninterrogatory as any I ever heard her make. She said, "Everybody's got to believe something."

206

Suddenly, out of nowhere, a new voice spoke. It said, "That is true, dear," and we all wheeled around to find that it was Brownie, of course. He'd come in through the front and was standing behind us in the doorway.

It was Brownie's voice and yet not Brownie's voice just as it was Brownie and yet not Brownie. It was Brownie grown twenty years older. He was leaning against the jamb with a silvery stubble on his chin and his clothes all wrinkled as though he had slept in them. It was Brownie without his teeth.

To come upon a man without his teeth is an unnerving business under any circumstances. It not only changes his face but changes all faces in more or less the same way so that, like mongoloids, every man without his teeth looks much like all other men without their teeth. My dentist Darius Bildabian has a habit of leaving his treatment doors open, and I have stumbled into more acquaintances than I care to remember in just such a state. But in Brownie's case the change was even more unnerving still because without his teeth he was without his smile. And Brownie *was* his smile. I never realized how much so until the grotesque and tragic moment when he tried to smile for me when he had nothing in the world to smile with. It was like seeing a man try to walk without legs.

Sharon said, "Brownie, what's happened to you?" and he said, "It's my teeth, dear. A third set is coming in so they don't fit anymore." Then you could see him steeling himself for what he had to say next.

"Babe's outside," he said. "He says if you all aren't out of here by noon, he'll get the sheriff."

I shudder to think what it must have cost Brownie to

bear such a message and how almost lethal a dose of life-ray Babe must have used to get him to bear it. He staggered as soon as the words were out, his face ashen, and then it was like that scene from *On the Waterfront* where Marlon Brando's brother pulls the gun on him and Marlon Brando goes so mumbly with grief and disappointment and embarrassment for his brother that the gun might as well not exist, much as Brownie might as well not have delivered his terrible message the way Sharon totally ignored it in her grief and disappointment and embarrassment. She helped him into a kitchen chair and hung over him like Mother herself. Brownie said, "It's nothing, dear. I just haven't had my breakfast yet."

I said, "We're your friends, Brownie. How could you ever side with him?" and he said, "He's got the life-ray, dear. He's given me a new lease on life."

Sharon said, "You look like death, Brownie."

Brownie said, "It's like Bert said. Everybody's got to believe in something or somebody."

I said, "Brownie, he goes around in drag and sets fire to shit houses." He was all but down for the count and yet even so I had the compulsion to use words like *shit* on him.

He said, "Maybe he's got reasons he can't tell us. He gets hearings sometimes he won't tell about to a soul. All I know is when he turns the life-ray on me, I can feel the cares just melt away."

Sharon said, "It's not like he just hits the bottle or cheats on his wife. They could send him up ten years for the things he's done."

Brownie said, "There's things about him I don't understand just like there were things about God.

You've just got to have faith, dear. It's like somebody calls you in the dark and you pick up and go even though you can't see where to put your foot. Scripture is full of dark places a man can't understand."

I said, "There was a time you could explain them without half trying, Brownie."

He said, "The trouble was I couldn't explain the dark places in myself, dear. I prayed 'Lead us not into temptation but deliver us from evil' for many years, and he never delivered me. It was something I could never understand."

I said, "You're a good man, Brownie, and if there's a heaven, you'll get an aisle seat. The trouble is you give up too easily."

"Oh don't think it was easy," he said, and said it in the windy dialect of the toothless with such sadness in it that for a while we just stayed there in silence.

Outside it had started to rain, a feathery grey rain with a grey mist rising. It fell on the roof of the hen house and on the hood of Babe's car, and I thought of it falling all over Poinsett—on Shaw Hill and shantytown, on Lola's Trailer Court. I pictured Jimmy Bob Luby in soiled diapers by the trailer window listening to it fall, the drops no more in number than the lives he had lived, had yet to live.

Sharon was the one to speak finally. She said, "You can tell that old fart I've got a letter proves the will's legal and it's my house. I'll give him twenty-four hours to get his moonflops out of here, and if he shows his ass around here after that, I'll blow it off."

A tear ran down Brownie's cheek. The kettle started to whistle. Callaway appeared in the doorway, as narrow and dark as a doorway himself. "Frumbo digga awning," he said. Then Gertrude Conover. She looked refreshed and ready for the worst. She picked Brownie's hand off the table where it lay and shook it. She said, "Stay for a coffee, Brownie. I've been watching Babe from upstairs. He is in a cataleptic trance."

Brownie again did the best he could in the way of a smile. It was like something ancient and unrecognizable in the back of the refrigerator. He said, "I'm feeling a little under the weather. I better not," and from the stove Bert said, "There's eggs ready?" said it more to Callaway than to anyone else. There were dark bloodstains on the front of Callaway's shirt from his last nosebleed, and he sat with his face turned away from her, his black chin in the V of his coral palms.

There was a single, sustained blast from Babe's car which someone else might have been sounding for all Babe so much as blinked an eye, sitting out there like laundry in the wet. Then he gave a short second blast, then another, and I could feel him doing the same grim things to me that he had already done to Callaway. There was nobody in the world that he was closer to in a way than Bert and Brownie, but Babe had fixed it so that Callaway couldn't bring himself to look at either of them.

Sharon said, "Do like I told you, Brownie. Tell him I've got a letter proves Bip's my daddy. Tell him to go to hell."

So Brownie headed off into the rain in his rumpled shorts and bobby-socks, and the rest of us sat down to watery scrambled eggs and bitter coffee, resisting the temptation to gawk out the window to see how Babe would react to Sharon's answer to his ultimatum. His trance seemed so profound that it was hard to think of his reacting much at all, hard to think of him as the same man who had done a dance of rage and despair on his brother's relics.

While we waited, Gertrude Conover said, "This is a sad business. Well, it is a mess. But think of it this way. If the great wheel is to keep turning, part of it must be turning downward so the rest of it can be turning upward. Downward, upward, sad things and happy things, it's all one. It's all just the wheel going round, round, round." Her gold bracelet rattled as she traced several revolutions in the air with her finger. She said, "My dear, the whole point is to get off the wheel. That is theosophy in a nutshell. It is also common sense."

I said, "It is also Ufology. Spacelift will carry us off to a better world."

"That would be only out of the frying-pan into the fire," Gertrude Conover said. "One world is as much part of the wheel as another part."

I said, "At least this one doesn't smell of stale piss."

Sharon said, "That's what you think."

I said, "At least they let you die in this one. It's not much, but it's something."

Gertrude Conover said, "Die and be born, die and be born. It's just back to the wheel again through the same old door. Death isn't all it's cracked up to be. It's like life that way."

She had a forkful of scrambled eggs she was about to eat but then lowered it slowly to her plate again. She said, "When I stood there in the twilight with Jimmy Bob in my arms, for a moment or two I felt neither life nor death could lay a finger on us. I will never forget it as long as I live. Neither life nor death. I suppose it was the peace that passeth all understanding. I could tell the baby felt it too."

Bert said, "You ever have any babies of your own, honey?"

Gertrude Conover said, "When I married Harold Conover, I was fifty and he was going on seventy three."

Sharon said, "They're getting out of the car."

They were. Callaway leapt to his feet and went to the window. He kept so far off to the side that from out-doors the most you could have seen of him was a single eye, a single sliver of bony black cheek. Brownie and Babe were standing in the rain discussing something, Babe had a large brown-paper bag in his arms. He was wearing his see-through raincoat, but he was bareheaded, his hair standing out in damp red spikes as it had the first time we'd met. Brownie gestured limply toward the house.

Callaway said, "Rootabaga mushseed. Alpha slope." He said, "Gunner flaymole. Mowdown. Limbo," dark, solemn words that clouded the pane with his breath. Beyond him I could see Babe and Brownie walking slowly out of sight around the front of the house.

Bert laid one hand lightly on Sharon's bare arm, and it occurred to me that it might be the first time she'd touched her that way since the day Bebb had taken her away in a blanket to turn over to Lucille where she lay on the sofa listening to Major Bowes. She said, "Don't be scared, honey? You got the letter." There was the sound of the front door opening, footsteps in the hall.

The wagons were drawn up in a circle, in other words,

every eye cocked toward where the attack would come from. There was a humming in the air. The refrigerator coming on? Saucers landing? The life-ray? My life was in my throat. Brownie was the first to appear on the horizon. He stood in the door with that one lens of his glasses cracked like a saucer. Babe pushed in by him. What landed was the brown-paper bag with a wig in it and a big, sweat-stained, polka-dot dress with rips under both of the arms. It landed in Bert's lap where Babe tossed it. The humming of the tracks as the locomotive steamed along its deadly way?

The womenfolk were steely-eyed and indomitable, not a green rose or a blue curl stirring. Sharon's thin smile was tight as a bowstring. Callaway and I stood our ground behind where they sat at the round table. Babe and Brownie had us surrounded. Babe said, "It's my house, rat? It's my wife, rat? The law's on my side, rat?" His words ricocheted past us as he stood there in his see-through raincoat seen through by all of us but as though it was a cause for pride instead of shame.

Bert had her wig out of the bag in seconds, slipping it on with her fingers inside to ease it down over her shiny scalp like a bathing cap. She said, "My dress is all tore?"

Babe said, "I'm giving you today to clear out. I'm giving you twenty-four hours to git." He was never more Bebbsian, that plump hypnotist, impersonator, space-traveler who had held his nose to the stink of eternity offering us time like prairie flowers. He was playing his pair of deuces like a royal flush. He said, "No hard feelings. I won't make trouble for your boy here if you go quiet. If Leo left you cash money, take it and welcome. All I want's what's mine by rat."

213

"It's mine," Sharon said. "It's mine to do something nice for Jesus with or any damn thing I want."

Babe said, "It's mine mine mine mine mine," a gibbering parody, his face all screwed up, his shoulders hunched to his ears. Then he said, "The trouble with Leo, he thought he was Jesus his ownself half the time. He preached the Kingdom like he was the king of it. That two-bit diploma factory, he turned out ministers like they were candy bars. All the miracles of Scripture, they looked like peanuts alongside his miracles," and Brownie said, "It's true, dear. I was laid out for dead in Knoxville, Tennessee, and Mr. Bebb raised me. He told me to stand up in Jesus's name, and I stood up."

Babe said, "Let me tell you about Jesus."

It was Jesus the spaceman I was prepared for, Jesus with a noseplug stepping out of his saucer to the rescue, and I think that was the Jesus Brownie was prepared for too. You could see he wasn't looking forward to it, but at least he knew he could live with it. It turned out to be another Jesus.

Babe said, "I know my Scripture same as Leo knew it. Why shouldn't I? We got it shoved down our throats like tonic from the time we could pee standing. Right there in the Gospel it reads, 'Jesus wept,' and if I had a nickel for every time they've preached on that one, I'd be riding around in a Cadillac sedan. Jesus, he was the best old weeper of all time. If they was to give a prize for weeping, he'd win the kewpie doll, hands down."

He said, "The sacred heart of Jesus. The R.C.s they've got them pictures of it looks like a tomato done up in barbwire. The world's in one hell of a way, and Jesus weeps till his sacred heart near to pops. Hell, he's been at it since the year one without a coffee break. There's miseries in this world enough to make a stone weep." He pulled out a dishtowel and rubbed his hair with it.

He said, "There's a pile-up on the interstate rips the tits off a teenage girl. There's old folks in nurse homes they don't even change their drawers when they let go in them. There's crooks and half-wits loose in the streets and phonecalls at midnight to wake folks up with awful things they never dreamed could happen, not to them anyways, six year old kids some pervert stuffed into a sack after they did things their own mother wouldn't recognize them."

Gertrude Conover had her head turned sideways as if one ear was all she could bear to listen with, and there were tears rolling down poor Brownie's cheeks that would have made even Jesus look to his laurels. Babe shied his horrors out like the plastic lids with Sunshine on them. He said, "They're starving and fighting and dying of cancers the whole world over, and all the weeping Jesus ever did since Lazarus hasn't helped more than a bucket of spit." His hair was a red feather duster from the rubbing, a fright wig. "You think I wouldn't believe if I could? You think that—Listen," he said, breaking in on himself. "Leo was all the time preaching hold tight to Jesus, hold tight to Jesus. It's like a drowning man holding tight to water. The day I'll believe is the day I see him coming across the waves with his hand stretched out. It's the day I hear him say, 'You look all wore out, Babe,' and I take a hold of his hand. Hell, there's been times I held my hand out in the dark till it went pins and

215

needles on me waiting for him, and he never come yet. I never seen him yet, and Leo Bebb never seen him either."

Gertrude Conover said, "How do you know what Leo Bebb saw?" and Babe said, "The dark and shameful things he done showed he was lost in the dark like the rest of us, that's how I know."

Gertrude Conover said, "Leo Bebb could see in the dark. He was never lost. Even blind, that man could see."

I stood there like a rube at a high-wire act until without warning the old acrobat had me up there with him. For the first time he raised his glance to me, said, "You ever seen Jesus, Antonio Parr?" He was close enough to smell as he said it, the smell of him rain, plastic, a whiff of peppermint. He was sucking on something. He blinked at me, and *you and me* his blink said. He said, "Father, Son, and Holy Smoke, you ever laid eyes on that crowd, Antonio Parr?"

I have read that men shot down in battle who've lived to tell the tale tell that there comes a moment when you rise high in the air above your own body and look down at where it lies on the ground as good as dead, and that's how it was in that kitchen when out of the blue Babe let me have it. I looked down and saw myself. I looked down at that familiar bald spot, that elongated, olive-skinned face, those caramel-colored eyes I got from my Italian mother, El Greco eyes as Miriam called them, rolled heavenward, glassy, brimming with whatever El Greco eyes brim with. Father, Son or Holy Smoke? fat Babe asks. His question smells of peppermint and rain.

216

The only answer I have is that I know what I've looked at but not what I've seen.

I have looked at my sister in a hospital room with storm-tinted windows and both legs in casts with a bar between them so she is a white A on a white bed. She smokes a cigarette, her hair tied back with a florist's ribbon. *Ciao, Antonio.* She says her doctor looks like Groucho Marx. She asks if I think dying is going some-place or just going out, like a match, and I am inspired to tell her how I have a fantasy in which Jesus is Don Giovanni, the great lover himself, with a little gold earring in one ear and an Errol Flynn smile as he runs Satan through with a sword and puts Death to rout. *Bene, bene, Antonio,* she says. For once I have said the right thing although I can be sure of nothing except that it's a thing I've said.

I have looked at Stephen Kulak who sits in my ninth grade class as I explain what irony is. It is saying one thing and meaning another thing, I say—two things. That doesn't give him any trouble but the idea that life can be ironic too does; so out of my Santa's pack I pull the example of a bride getting killed on her way to a wedding. En route to a fresh start she runs into a dead-end—two things—and in a classroom with the Pledge of Allegiance on the walls and Christmas scotchtaped to the windows I look at Stephen Kulak's face falling like Rome to the barbarians. He knows what irony is.

And I have looked at Lucille. Like an extinct species, half smashed on Tropicanas, she teeters up the aisle of Open Heart in her Aimee Semple MacPherson gauze because in the pulpit Bebb is opening his heart so wide she is terrified that he may at any moment pull out of it like a rabbit from a hat Bertha Stredwig in her young beauty on the Shaw Hill, the brawl in Knoxville with his twin pounding him till one eye's never been right since.

It was Gertrude Conover who came to my rescue finally. She reached out her hand and pointed it at Babe. It was an old, bony hand with liver spots on it and a glittering diamond. If it had been a gun and she'd fired it, it would have gotten him right on his left nipple. She said, "You always have to get back at your brother, Babe. You always have to go him one better. It is your main trouble. He believes in the Mystery—well, more than believes, he keeps riding it back into the world like Pegasus—and so you believe in saucers, hardware. If he believed in hardware, you would believe in the Mystery, or let on you did. Anything to spite him. You were well named. You are a babe. The Mystery is deep and holy, and you have baby eyes that see only the nasty surfaces of things and the shiny toys in the sky."

Babe said, "Gertrude Conover, my brother had the gift of gab and a zipper he couldn't keep zipped. He made good business out of Jesus, but deep down he believed the same as me."

Gertrude Conover said, "I'm afraid you would have a hard time convincing me you know what Leo Bebb believed."

Babe said, "Then how's if I let him convince you his ownself?"

I thought for a moment that it was Callaway who spoke next but then found it was Brownie doing the best he could with only gums to do it with. He said, "Babe's going to give us a hearing, dear." And he was right.

Babe opened his mouth as wide as if Bildabian was about to work on a back molar and aimed it at us like a mortar. I was ready for anything. I was ready for the voice of Bebb himself speaking of how it would be when the Lone Ranger came riding into the world with justice on one hip and mercy on the other. I was ready for some Martian message to the effect that Bebb like Babe believed in nothing more hopeful than hardware or anything more mysterious than Mars, that the Gospel was just what he hid the dark truth behind, the one shamefulness he could not bear to bare. I was ready for anything except what happened, which was for a few moments nothing.

The tea kettle was whistling softly like a man through his teeth. It was still raining outside. Babe raised his hands to his gaping jaws as if to knead sound out of them. His face flushed dark, his eyes watered. He was giving it all he had, every muscle straining. But there was no message from Mars, no credo from Bebb, only the silence of a radio turned on between stations, dead air. And only then the unmistakable sound of a dry, weightlifter's fart.

Somebody might have laughed, God knows. Babe might have carried the day if he had, if he'd let the fart be his final word to us, the innermost, outermost word of outerspace. But he didn't, only closed his mouth far enough to say, "Sometimes it don't work worth a damn," then closed it the rest of the way.

I suppose somebody might have wept. Possibly Jesus.

Instead nobody did much of anything for a while till finally Sharon did. She reached down into her jeans and pulled out Bebb's letter. She said, "Read it and weep, Babe," and handed it to him—"Dear One, I went and picked her up today . . . Luce has fixed on giving her the name of Sharon . . . Farewell, my own dear heart . . . Remember me."

Babe took it and tipped it toward the light. His lips moved as he read it. When he had finished, he said, "This here don't prove a thing I didn't know. It proves your daddy was a fornicator and a four-flusher. It proves you were got in shame and born to grief."

Sharon said, "It proves this is my kitchen you're letting them in."

He said, "Honey, it don't prove shit," and tore the letter in two.

What happened then is this. As Babe tore the letter, Brownie jumped up to grab it from him and Babe tried to keep it out of his reach by holding it up as high as he could above his head. Dancing around on his toes, Brownie made a number of unsuccessful snatches at it as if Babe was the school bully who'd run off with his hat. Or they could have been dancing together, because Babe was dancing around too a little, trying to keep away from Brownie. Then Babe brought his hand down hard with the letter in it, and hand, letter, arm, something, must have caught Brownie on the side of the head en route because he staggered backwards a few steps and his glasses went spinning off across the linoleum. Then, still on his toes, Brownie himself went spinning across the linoleum. Only he did it in slow motion.

An MGM stunt man couldn't have done it better,

shot through the chest by Brian Donlevy on the edge of a cliff. In his short pants with his hairy, pale legs and bobby socks, Brownie revolved as slow as a dream, his bare arms crooked out to either side. His sunset shirt was all purples and reds. His face was colorless. He was trying to say something but all that came out were syllables of air. His legs buckled and he went down on his knees near the stove. He grabbed on to the stove with one hand, but one by one his fingers lost hold. He lay on the kitchen floor with his mouth open and his glance fixed on the ceiling. There was a coil of flypaper hanging down from the ceiling, but whatever he was looking at, if he was looking at anything, it wasn't the flypaper.

Finally he got a word out. Sharon and I were both down there with him by then and we both heard it, but the only dictionary to look up what it meant in would be a rhyming dictionary because without his choppers he couldn't handle the initial consonant and only the vowel sound came through.

Hear? He wanted to hear something, or for us to hear something he was hearing, or to hear with him that there wasn't anything to hear?

Or *here,* for all we could tell—not anywhere else in time or space or outerspace but just here, this place, this time, this intersection and meeting of many ways. If there was any answer to find that was worth a damn, the only place to find it finally was your own place, not there, or there, or there, but only here, stretched out in a kitchen in Poinsett, South Carolina, if it came to that, with your glasses shattered on the linoleum and your smile in a bureau drawer. *Here.*

Or even *beer* maybe. It's possible that all poor

Brownie was trying to get across was that he wanted to take a little something once more while he still could, something to wet his lips with and keep his courage up.

But we came up with something else finally, Sharon and I. Nobody can live comfortably for long with uncertainty, and for comfort's sake if not accuracy's even the most cut-and-dried historian ends his history with a period instead of a colon or a question mark or a little trailing row of dots. . . . So, discarding all the other possibilities, the one we finally put our money on was the one that seemed to have the most of Brownie in it, and later on that day, when the dust settled a little and things quieted down and people started asking about the particulars, we told everybody that the last word we heard him speak there on the floor by Bert's stove was *dear*.

CHAPTER FOURTEEN

I FOUND I HAD to phone somebody what had happened if only to help get it through to myself, and since there was no next of kin, Mother presumably having long since passed, to use Bert's term, I phoned John Turtle at the Redpath Ranch. He arrived the next day with his friends.

He arrived at Spartanburg by chartered plane and brought his friends out from there in a pair of sky-blue Granadas complete with air-conditioning, tape decks, and whitewall tires. He brought Harry Hocktaw, Harry Hocktaw who could have passed for Jack Oakie any day, more Eskimo than Indian with his swelling cheeks and sparse, pussycat whiskers. He also brought the newly-weds, Buck Badger and Rose Trionka Badger and Rose's mother Bea. Herman Redpath's cousin Seahorn Redpath also came. Instead of returning to Laguna Beach after the wedding, he had apparently lingered on at the ranch, and having him come was almost like having Herman Redpath come himself. He was a good head shorter and as silent a man as his cousin had been a non-stop talker, but otherwise the resemblance was striking—the same narrow arrowhead of a face, the same high-bridged tomahawk of a nose. And last but not least, Maudie Redpath was there in her hundred and twelfth year looking as though the dance that was supposed to turn her into a blackbird had worked at last. She wore a black dress with feathery black wings for sleeves, and all you could see of her face through the wrinkles was a pair of glittering eyes and a hooked, seed-cracking beak. The Joking Cousin himself lifted her out of one of the Granadas into her collapsible wheelchair and wheeled her through Bert's chickens with the red, white and blue streamers a little the worse for wear but still laced through the spokes.

They came to escort Brownie's body back to Holy Love, but there were preliminaries to attend to first. The Spartanburg undertaker raised all kinds of objections, but John Turtle prevailed, and they were finally allowed in to wherever it was they had Brownie laid out. John Turtle, Buck Badger, and Harry Hocktaw were the ones who worked on him, and though I made a point of not asking about it, they told Sharon he was an honorary member of the tribe and they had done the same kind of thing for him that they had done for Herman Redpath and others before him. She said, "I suppose they put butter on his legs and salt on his tongue and up his nose and ears and up his rear end to keep the evil spirits out. Jesus. I wonder did John Turtle take a leak on him like he did on old Herman. I was going to ask him, but I didn't. I didn't want to know about it either way." So I asked him.

I said, "When Herman Redpath was in his box, you took a leak on him, John Turtle, and Bebb told me afterwards that it was what kept him from getting lost on his way to the Happy Hunting Ground. Don't ask me how he knew. Did you do the same for Brownie?"

I never saw John Turtle laugh harder, his gold-framed front teeth flashing at me like fire. His black hair was plastered down like the watersoak in the old ads, and he had on a checked sports jacket with padded shoulders and saddle shoes with the white parts so freshly whitened that you could smell the banana oil. He said, "You kill me, Cousin. Brownie get lost with all that aftershave on him? He don't need Joking Cousin to find his way. He need just one thing, and I give it to him. No sweat."

I said, "You want me to guess?" It is impossible to talk with a Joking Cousin very long without becoming his stooge.

He said, "Carraway found it."

"Callaway," I said.

He said, "Halloway found it in Brownie's bag. My, the pretty things old Brownie have in there. I took and give it to him before they shut the box anyhow." He cocked his head to one side and stared at me with a glazed smile. He said, "How you been, Cousin? Getting much lately?"

I said, "You wouldn't mean his teeth, would you?"

He said, "Once we get his mouth open, they slip in like nobody's business." He placed his right hand on my left shoulder. He said, "We shine them up real nice first. They look like a million dollars."

I said, "You didn't happen to notice if he had any real teeth coming in, did you?"

He said, "You crazy?"

I said, "Well, he'll rest easier now, John Turtle. It was a nice thing you did."

He said, "Nobody's going to slam the door on a nice smile like that."

I said, "Maybe you should have taken a leak on him too just to make sure."

He placed his left hand on my right shoulder so his arms were crossed between us and closed his eyes. He said, "Just a little one for the road maybe," and bent his head forward until his brow touched the place where his arms crossed. His hair smelled of nutmeg and olive oil. He dug his fingers into my shoulders so hard that it brought tears to my eyes.

I suppose that as with Herman Redpath they painted designs on him too, a red one for the earth and a blue one for the sky, and hung a deerskin pouch around his neck with things in it he'd need for the journey like an extra supply of aftershave maybe and a fresh Harry Truman shirt. Possibly they even put in what was left of his glasses although, as Saint Paul said in another of Bebb's favorite passages, "Now we see through a glass darkly, but then face to face, Antonio," so maybe glasses would have been to load him down unnecessarily. But the important thing, of course, was the teeth. Maybe they weren't his own—I was as relieved by the knowledge that the life-ray hadn't worked as I suppose poor Brownie was demolished by it—but they were his by adoption, his by grace, and if he ever made it to where he was going, I feel sure that if for no other reason they let him in for the sake of his million dollar smile.

It was a heart attack that killed him, not Babe, but it was Babe, of course, who brought it on by loading more on him than his heart could handle. He'd had Bebb shot out from under him and then Jesus. He'd given up Holy Love because he couldn't make the rough places of Scripture smooth any more even for himself and then took to taking a little something to help fill the empty places Jesus and the Scriptures and Bebb had left behind them. Then he'd latched on to Babe only to discover the terrible truth about him at Lola's Trailer Court. I suppose it was because of his teeth as much as anything that he stuck with Babe after that. New every morning was the love that Brownie's dream of a complete new set did prove, to take liberties with the old hymn. He would search around with his tongue until he convinced himself that he could feel them starting to poke through somewhere and then he would know that even if Jesus was only a spaceman, at least Mother was home and maybe Babe had his weaknesses but who hadn't. But then Babe tore the letter up. "Honey, it don't prove shit," he said, and tore it in two and Brownie's last hope with it.

It was the end of him, and yet it was also in a way the

227

beginning—two things, as I might have explained it to Stephen Kulak. It killed him, but it also brought him to life for a few wild minutes and in a way that I think would have made Bebb take back all his remarks about how he let his life slip out sideways. Dancing around on his toes trying to snatch the letter back may not have looked like much, but for Brownie it was Little Big Horn and San Juan Hill. And only then did his heart attack him, flattening him out on the linoleum to be sure but only after he'd made that one last, first, and only stand. And routed Babe in the bargain.

An elderly doctor with a white face and hair and pink, rabbity eyes drove out from Poinsett to pronounce him dead, and while he was checking him over where Callaway and I had placed him on the horsehair sofa, Sharon went upstairs and found Babe. It was her house and he was her uncle, and she went alone to find him although I had offered to go with her. She found him just inside the door of the little varnished room where Bert kept her treasure. She said he was standing there like a statue staring into space with his mouth open and a flap of his raincoat hanging down where it had gotten torn in the scuffle. The remains of the letter were still in his hand, and she said he hardly seemed to notice it when she took them out of his hand as you would from a child's. She said she didn't make a big scene of it but just stepped into his line of vision so she was sure he noticed her and in a quiet, grim tone said, "Babe, if you don't start packing your things, I'm going to phone the troopers and say you killed him same as if you did it with a gun. I'm going to press manslaughter charges and get you jailed quicker than you can say moonflops." She said to me,

"The crazy thing is I think he was almost grateful to me, Bopper. I think the poor slob was so shook up he was glad when somebody told him what the hell to do."

As Stephen Kulak is bound to discover someday, the effect of death on a household is not unlike the effect of a wedding—the same comings and goings, the same suspension of routine, the sense of holiday almost and of history, the gathering of the clan. The doctor came. The undertaker came with his two assistants in dark leisure suits and carried Brownie out through the Uforium on a stretcher with aluminum poles. I phoned John Turtle in Houston, and when he said he'd be flying in with his friends, Sharon in one of her rare flights of domesticity started worrying about feeding them and got Callaway to drive into town with her to help bring back provisions. Bert said, "Life's got to go on?" and went on herself about her usual chores, walking out through the drizzle with a raincoat over her head to feed her heekies, cleaning up after our unfinished breakfast, mopping up the red mud the undertakers had tracked in. I don't think any of us shed a tear for Brownie that day, not that there weren't tears to shed but simply that there were so many other things to get out of the way first.

What Gertrude Conover did was go sit in the front parlor with the door shut. She said, "The first few hours when you die are always the hardest. The gods, the bodhisattvas, the what-have-yous positively swarm about you. They are all trying to sell you the new birth that will suit you best. They are trying to be helpful, most of them, but it is like Nassau Street on Reunion weekend. I will sit in here and try to send a little good karma Brownie's way for the voyage. If you can get it through, it sometimes makes the difference between going tourist or first class for them."

And then with her hand on the doorknob, she said, "They shouldn't let death happen around people my age. It is like doing a *pas de chat* in front of a cripple." Then she shut the door between us.

All the time these things were going on, Babe was getting ready to leave, almost, as Sharon said, as though he was grateful for something to do, as though it had been his own idea in the first place. He made a number of phone calls from his office. He ran up and down stairs. He dragged suitcases out of the varnished room. He packed them, and you could hear him moving things around in the Uforium. He had destroyed his marriage and he had been accused of murder and he was being driven out of his own house, but if indeed it had been the day of a wedding instead of a death, it was as if Babe was the bride getting ready to set out on a new life. Sometime around the middle of the afternoon he called out to Sharon and me that he was leaving and we went into the Uforium to see him go. It was both the least and the most that we could do.

He had on his best clothes—a skimpy-looking dark suit that grabbed him under the arms with the collar of his shirt spread out over the suit collar and on his head a shiny little straw fedora with a feather in the band. He could have been bald for all you could see with the hat on, and that plus the tightness of the suit made him look so much like his brother in the dim, extraterrestrial light that I would have gasped if I'd had a gasp left in me by then.

He said, "I'm leaving most of this stuff behind, I

won't need it. I'm taking the space-suit and a couple of moonrocks and this." It was the collander with the wires threaded through it. He said, "You can have the rest. Maybe Jesus can use it if he moves in."

Sharon said, "Nobody here's got a use for it, Babe."

"Don't you bother yourself about it anyhow," he said.

He said, "There's no manslaughter charge would stick worth a damn because there was no man here got slaughtered. I'm leaving because I got the biggest hearing I ever heard yet. I got it in the store room up there when you busted in."

He said, "Antonio, spacelift's coming only not to Shaw Hill it isn't. Once it was Shaw Hill but it's not Shaw Hill any more. There's things they've found about Shaw Hill they wouldn't soil their feet with it. They've picked them a new place, and that's where I'm heading out for. I've been on the phone, and there's a few of them that's coming with me. S.O.S., that's Save Our Skins. Antonio, looks like if you want your skin saved, you better jump aboard. There's always room for one more."

For something around twenty or thirty seconds, I actually considered it. Then I said, "Send us a postcard when you get there, Babe."

He said, "There's bats in the attic, and the sump backs up. The clapboard's all dozey under the shingles. Old Leo, he didn't leave you the Ritz Hotel when he left it to you." He pulled one of the shades back and glanced out at the house as if to confirm what he'd said about it. The rainlight turned his face silver. He said, "What are you fixing to do with it anyway?"

"Fumigate first," Sharon said.

He took it in silence except for some little noise at the back of his throat, let the shade fall back in place so his face wasn't silver anymore. He said, "Promise me one thing, hear?" He said, "Long as she wants to, let Bert stay. I don't know where else in the world she'd find to go."

Sharon said, "Jesus, Babe. You think I'd turn her out?"

He said, "She turned you out once."

Sharon said, "Because you wouldn't let her keep me. She had her one pitiful little fling, and you set out to ruin her life from then on."

Babe said, "Your daddy was the one that ruined her life. He ruined both our lives."

Sharon said, "I don't think he ever got over it. I think every crazy, half-ass thing he ever did was on account of it. Like in Miami, flashing it like that. He was trying to get it out where somebody could tell him it wouldn't count against him forever."

"Why shouldn't it count against him forever?" Babe said. There were a couple of Sunshine frisbies on the windowsill, and he picked them up absently and dropped them in the carton where he had the charred shoulderpads and the collander. He said, "Take a man that cheats on his own brother like that, he deserves what he gets."

Sharon said, "It must give you a sour stomach, all that spite you've got."

Babe said, "We slept in the same bed till we were twelve. We told each other the secrets of our heart. We held onto each other in the dark for comfort. There was a time it was him and me against the world." He half picked up the charred shoulder pad by one shoulder and let it drop again. He said, "I loved the sonofabitch."

Sharon said, "Well, it's over and done with." Between where she was standing and Babe, the table with the relief map stood, the different colored pins, the question mark. She glanced down and with one finger traced the course of a blue stream. She said, "Bip was a lonesome man his whole life. He could have used somebody to hold onto in the dark for comfort."

Babe was staring straight ahead, his mouth snapped shut on its hinges, his nostrils slightly distended as if he was humming something under his breath. He said, "I used to figure he'd come back someday. I took to watching for him nights. I'd sit out under a tree. Talk about your lonesome, I'd sit there half the night sometimes. It's when I commenced seeing UFOS. You stare into the dark long enough, there's no telling what you'll start seeing."

He said, "The first time one of them landed, I thought it was him that got out. I saw a creature standing there looking up at the window for all the world like him the way his bald head shone in the moonlight like a silver hat. I whispered out, 'It's me. Babe. I won't shoot.' Hell, it wasn't me he wanted. Night after night, every shadow moved I thought was him and every sound of the night, a owl or some little creature in the dry leaves."

Like Bebb he had a handkerchief in his breast pocket with the points carefully arranged. Only his mouth moved. He said, "It was Bert he wanted so I took to going around other places nights he might think it was Bert out looking for him in that pitiful wig of hers with her heart and spirit broken, both, from the time he broke

233

them. I took to doing damnfool things. A man can't only wait but so long for something to happen that never happens before he starts acting like a damn fool. The things I did never hurt a living soul, but they'd have locked me up if they'd ever caught me."

Sharon said, "You're lucky they never locked you up, Babe."

There was nothing more to say then, and none of us tried to say anything to pretend there was. Babe picked up his carton and stood there holding it against his stomach with both hands.

He said, "Tell her goodby for me, hear? Tell her I never meant her any harm." As things turned out, we never had to deliver the message.

When he got out to where he had his car parked in front of the house, Bert was there beside it in the rain. She had a plastic bandanna tied under her chin and a raincoat that almost reached to the ground. She had two big bags with her that Callaway must have helped her out with, one of them with a piece of clothesline around it. I remained standing in the doorway, but Sharon ran out. Even at that distance, you could see the awkwardness between them. Bert took a step backward, almost tripping over her raincoat. Sharon seemed to be saying something. Bert put both her hands out toward her daughter's face. Then they reached out and clumsily embraced in the rain. It was coming down hard by then, dimpling the puddles in the road and running off the wings and beaks of the flamingos.

When Sharon got back to the house, her face and hair dripping wet, all of her, she said, "She says I have you, Bopper, but Babe doesn't have anybody. She says she'll send me a card when they get where they're going. It must be some kind of a record, Bopper. I finally find my own mother, and a couple of days later she takes off for outerspace. Maybe I ought to try the spray can instead of the roll-on." She was so cold and miserable I don't think she could tell any better than I could whether rain was the only thing her face was wet with.

It was the next morning that the Indians arrived in their sky-blue Granadas, and though John Turtle, Harry Hocktaw and Buck Badger soon took off again to open negotiations with the Spartanburg undertaker, that still left the three women together with Seahorn Redpath hanging around the house with us at a time when we were least equipped to deal with them. We had to pull ourselves together for the trip back to Sutton for one thing, and we had to decide what to do with the house now that Sharon had successfully taken possession of it for another. The question of what to do with it for Jesus had gotten lost in the question of what to do with it at all—to rent it, sell it, lock it up and get somebody to keep an eye on it for us till we thought of something else to do. Selling it and giving the money to some cause that Jesus would find congenial was the most tempting because it was simple and final, and yet, as always before, it struck us as something less than what Bebb had had in mind. It was too pallid, too un-Bebbsian, so we kept hashing the thing over while at the same time packing up and trying to keep the Indians out of our hair.

Seahorn Redpath and old Maudie were no problem. Their function seemed mainly ceremonial, and they spent their time in the parlor sitting at opposite ends of the horsehair sofa under the oval photograph of Bebb's grandparents with their Sunday suits and goiterish stares. We looked in on them occasionally. Maudie was in her black plumage with her feet hardly touching the floor, and Seahorn Redpath had his hands folded in his lap and a broad-brimmed Panama on his head. Neither of them said a word. Once we thought we heard signs of distress, a high-pitched, piping sound that came in short bursts like a bosun's whistle, but it turned out to be only Maudie Redpath singing a song that I remembered from a Christmas eve I spent once at the ranch. I was told at the time that it was a song that was supposed to restore potency, and I wondered if this time it could possibly be Brownie she had in mind. In any case she did not say anything to us but just kept on singing and Seahorn Redpath didn't say anything either. He had shifted from the sofa to a squatting position on the floor. He kept moving his head slowly to the right and then back again as if something slow and solemn was passing by in front of him. Bea Trionka and Rose, on the other hand, seemed to be everywhere at once and into everything. They went into rooms and peered into closets. They made themselves countless cups of instant coffee and used the one toilet constantly. In the Uforium they burned something that smelled like hair, and when I asked them about it, Bea Trionka said, "Of course it smelled like hair," and Rose said, "What you expect it to smell like. Aftershave?" hunching up her shoulders and putting her hand over her mouth. The way she had her hair arranged, a thick loop of it almost covered one eye, the other one brimming with whatever the expression was that she was using her hand to hide.

John Turtle called us from Spartanburg where the

undertaker was giving him a hard time about letting them in to do what they'd come to do for Brownie. He said the undertaker wanted to speak to us, and I was the one he spoke to. In a voice like Lester Maddox he said they had no embalmer's license and no respect for the dead and that one of them had some kind of a rattle he kept shaking with beans inside. He had already upset one funeral with it, and there was another funeral coming up that he was going to upset too. I said they were Brownie's friends and parishioners and maybe it would be best all round if he would just let them get on with it and then be on their way. In the background, as he paused for thought, I could hear the sound of Harry Hocktaw's rattle—chick chicka, chunk-chunk-chicka— and then finally, the undertaker gave in. For the dozenth time at least I could hear one of the Trionkas flush the can upstairs. One of Bert's roosters crowed. Then almost as soon as I'd hung it up, the phone rang, and it was my nephew Tony calling from a world farther away than Mars.

He said some independent film producer had seen a couple of the ads he was in and they wanted to run a screen test on him. With Laura working at the dentist's every day, he couldn't set it up till we came back, so if we would make it back as soon as we could, it would be a big help. He said, "Jesus, Tono. I just hope it's not one of these porn deals," and I said I hoped it wasn't too and we'd try to get started the next day if everything worked out. Then he put my son Bill on for a few minutes. Bill said, "A mouse got drowned in the toilet during Archie Bunker," and I said, "Well, I guess there are worse ways." In Spartanburg by then they had probably already started to put the salt in Brownie's nose and ears.

It was Gertrude Conover who solved the problem of the house, and like all great solutions—the wheel, the ripple in a hairpin—it was simplicity itself. She said, "My dear, you can give it to the Lubys," and we did. *Give* is perhaps not the right word—it remained Sharon's house but was theirs to look after, live in, report to us on, exorcise, debrief, hallow. It was surprisingly easy to arrange, people who live in mobile homes being more mobile than other people. And *Lubys* is not the right word either, of course—Jimmy Bob would be more accurate.

We did not leave the next day, as I told Tony I hoped we would because John Turtle insisted we be there for the send-off at the airport, and all in all I'm glad we didn't miss it. Harry Hocktaw and Buck Badger wheeled Brownie in his box, and the women walked behind with Seahorn Redpath pushing Maudie in her collapsible chair. John Turtle sang a song as the box went slowly up into the plane on a hoist. He stood behind little Seahorn Redpath with his arms around his neck and sang,

> *"Seahorn Redpath,*
> *Redpath from the sea,*
> *Sail old Brownie on to he.*
> *Red sail in the sunset,*
> *Oh red path in the sky,*
> *We all coming by and by*
> *You don't got no cause to cry.*

It could have been a lot worse.

We did not leave the next day but we left the day after the next, and the last thing I saw before we drove off was Jimmy Bob. Ruby and her husband were standing in the doorway with the other children crowded around them to wave goodbye, but Jimmy Bob had staggered out a few steps in front of them. He stood by the white tractor tire with the nasturtiums in it. His rubber pants were full as usual. His flat little eyes were still, but he was pumping his fat arms up and down in the air. "Bye bye bye bye," he called out to us, only it came out "Ba ba ba ba" in short, flat bleats. He started lurching forward as if to follow us, but Ruby caught him up around the middle, and he hung there over her arms bleating as we pulled out toward shantytown in the brutalized Continental with Callaway at the wheel.

Gertrude Conover said, "Well, there is nothing nicer you could have done for Jesus than that," and I said, "Maybe that's who that was out there with his rubber pants filled," and Sharon said, "I guess if he had rubber pants he'd fill them like everybody else."

Gertrude Conover said, "No. These always-returners, they never do anything like anybody else. They keep on returning until the last blade of grass has achieved cosmic consciousness. They keep coming back until a' the seas gang dry, my dear, till a' the seas gang dry." She craned around to give one last wave through the back window. She had her white gloves on for the first time since she had used them for protection against moon-germs. She said, "And I will love thee still, my dear, till a' the seas gang dry."

Then Callaway almost put us through the windshield braking for a yellow shantytown dog that ran out into the red clay road to menace us. Callaway turned around to look at us from under the visor of his green Agway cap and spoke the second word I ever heard him speak that I was sure I understood. The first was the number sixty-two when he was counting the freight cars the day we drove into Poinsett, and the second, after just missing the dog, was "Life." He pronounced it "Laff," flashing his teeth at us as if it was the best and oldest joke in the world. I don't know what he meant by it, though I suppose it had to do with the dog's narrow escape.

The same dog turned up in a dream I had that night in the Monticello Hotel in Charlottesville where we broke our trip on the ride home. The scene was the same as the terrible picture in Brownie's motel room of the sunlit millpond with the mill reflected in it and the boy sitting on the grassy bank fishing with his dog beside him. The dog was the shantytown dog, and the boy was Brownie. I wasn't myself a participant in the dream, only an observer, so there wasn't any chance to speak to Brownie or even to wave at him across the water, but I noticed to my relief that his smile was firmly back in place where John Turtle had put it. The dream didn't leave me feeling sad and neglected the way dreams about the dead usually do because no matter how well you once knew them, they have very little time for you when they meet you in dreams and generally seem in a great rush to get on with whatever it is they've got to do next. It was essentially a comic dream, not accidentally comic like a moment in real life, but comic on purpose like a Laurel and Hardy two-reeler.

Instead of Laurel and Hardy, it was Bebb and Babe, and they were floating on the pond side by side in the rowboat, each with an oar in his hands. They were both wearing straw boaters like a pair of vaudeville hoofers, both in their shirtsleeves with the sleeves rolled up. They weren't rowing anyplace, just resting their oars, and beyond them, on the far bank, the trees faded away into the golden haze. Brownie wasn't paying any attention to them, and after a while one of the brothers picked up something and tossed it at him, possibly a moonrock. When it splashed into the water, Brownie glanced up, and that was the signal for Babe and Bebb to start their act.

One of them started pulling on his oar and the other one started pushing on his, and the result was that instead of moving forward, of course, the boat started going around in a circle. Harder and harder they rowed, and faster and faster the boat went round. Their fat faces were flushed with excitement and effort, and sweat was rolling down from under their straw hats. Brownie set down his pole and gathered the dog into his lap. His smile was never more radiant even without his glasses to give it intensity. The boat spun so fast you could no longer make out what it was or who was in it, and like the tigers running around the tree in *Little Black Sambo* until they turn to butter, the oars, the oarsmen, their yellow straw boaters, all of it melted together and became part of the sunlight on the pond and the haze in the woods. When I looked back for Brownie he had gone, and the dog stood alone on the bank barking. Brownie was in the pond. He was already up to his chest in it, and before long only his head was above the surface as he waded out farther. His head looked like a beachball floating along in the water, and I laughed so hard at the ridiculous sight of it that I woke myself up with tears in my eyes.

*　　*　　*

"Tie a yellow ribbon round the old oak tree" was the
song that was going strong that summer, and when we
finally pulled into Sutton around supper time the next
day, having parted company with Gertrude Conover and
Callaway in Princeton and made the rest of the journey
in our own car, Bill and some friends of his with the song
in mind had gone to town on the homemade wooden
mobile I'd carpentered years before and hung up with
Tony's help from a tripod in the back yard—a great
unwieldy thing, basically A-shaped, of dowels and knobs
and lathing which year after year of kids and weather
and birddroppings was considerably the worse for wear
but still standing. When they had run out of yellow
ribbon, they had used whatever else they could lay their
hands on including enough yellow toilet paper to stretch
to Poinsett and back, and there it was when they led us
out to it, gotten up, as Sharon said, like a whorehouse
Christmas tree.

The sign on it said WELCOME HONE, that last little leg
of the last M missing because my son Bill either didn't
remember about it or had run out of steam by then
stringing all that toilet paper around. It seemed oddly
fitting. It was good to get home, but it was home with
something missing or out of whack about it. It wasn't
much, to be sure, just some minor stroke or serif, but
even a minor stroke can make a major difference, to
which I can hear Brownie saying, "There is a sermon in
that, dear," as he used to say in the days when he was
still preaching sermons instead of resting in peace in the
shadow of Holy Love in Houston or doing whatever else

242

he may be doing, wherever else he may be doing it.

To this day I cannot see my niece and former student Laura Fleischman Blaine without J. Alfred Prufrock's pair of ragged claws scuttling across my heart at the thought of days that might have been, of days that used to be. My namesake Tony's screentest turned out to be a smasher, and he went into the making of films which, if not technically hard core, are apparently close enough to it so that there are times when even he, as he likes to put it, isn't sure whether he's coming or going. I've never seen one of them, and I have no immediate plans to, but Sharon has seen them all and has gone on record, as she likes to put it, that he's really got something. I don't know how my sister Miriam would have felt about it, but I suspect she might have gotten a kick out of it. "You stay awake," were the last words she ever spoke to him the day I took him and his brother Chris to the hospital to say goodbye to her, and there is no question about his having done that. Besides, as I remind myself, it is a living.

WELCOME HONE the sign said, and I can't help thinking again of Gideon and Barak, of Samson and David and all the rest of the crowd that I had mentioned to Brownie once, who, because some small but crucial thing was missing, kept looking for it come hell or high water wherever they went till their eyes were dim and their arches fallen. And to think of them is to think of Babe too wherever he went off to with his transistorized teeth and his faithful Bert, and of Gertrude Conover letting Beethoven wash back over her under the stars at Revonoc. In the long run I suppose it would be to think of everybody if you knew enough about them to think straight: of Jimmy Bob Luby's father even, with the mean-looking, caved-in upper lip—who knows what far bank he wades toward in his dreams. And of Jimmy Bob too, doubled up over his mother's arm like a small, soiled pillow.

And of course I also think of myself, as every day I leave HONE to teach track and irony to the young only to come back again to make amends if I can, to make peace, make love when I can. I think of Antonio Parr with his glassy El Greco eyes rolled heavenward like a fish on cracked ice in a fishstore window.

"The weight of this sad time we must obey," says dull, dutiful Edgar at the end of Act Five, "Speak what we feel, not what we ought to say," and by and large I have tried to do that in this account of my life and times, my own search, I suppose, for whatever it is we search for in Poinsett, South Carolina, and Sutton, Connecticut, for whatever it is that is always missing. I am not sure I have ever seen it even from afar, God knows, and I know I don't have forever to see it in either. Already, if I make the mistake of listening, I can hear a dim humming in the tracks, Time's wingéd chariot hurrying near, as Andrew Marvell said to his coy mistress. But to be honest I must say that on occasion I can also hear something else too—not the thundering of distant hoofs, maybe, or *Hi-yo, Silver. Away!* echoing across the lonely sage, but the faint chunk-chunk of my own moccasin heart, of the Tonto afoot in the dusk of me somewhere who, not because he ought to but because he can't help himself, whispers *Kemo Sabe* every once in a while to what may or may not be only a silvery trick of the failing light.

FREDERICK BUECHNER

Frederick Buechner was born in New York City. He was educated at Lawrenceville School, Princeton University, and Union Theological Seminary. In 1958 he was ordained to the Presbyterian ministry. He has written nine novels and a number of works of non-fiction including two volumes of meditations (The Magnificent Defeat and The Hungering Dark), The Alphabet of Grace (delivered as the Nobel Lectures at Harvard) and Wishful Thinking: A Theological ABC. The Lyman Beecher Lectures that he delivered this year at Yale are soon to be published as Telling the Truth: The Gospel as Tragedy, Comedy and Fairy Tale. He lives in Vermont with his wife and three children.